S0-BEX-216

Nothing Sacred

Nothing Sacred

Based on *Fathers and Sons*
by Ivan Turgenev

George F. Walker

c. 1

The Coach House Press Toronto

Great North Artists Management, Inc.
350 Dupont Street
Toronto, Ontario, Canada M5R 1V9

Cover photo: Michael Riley as Arkady (left) and
Robert Bockstael as Bazarov in the CentreStage Company
production of *Nothing Sacred* at Toronto's St. Lawrence
Centre, January 1988.

The punctuation of this play carefully adheres to
the author's instructions.

Published with the assistance of the Canada Council
and the Ontario Arts Council.

Canadian Cataloguing in Publication Data

Walker, George F., 1947–
     Nothing sacred: based on Fathers and sons
by Ivan Turgenev.

A play.
ISBN 0-88910-331-3

I. Turgenev, Ivan Sergeevich, 1818-1883. Fathers and sons.
II. Title.

PS8595.A44N68 1988 C812'.54 C88-093848-X
PR9199.3.W34N68 1988

**To Bill Glassco
and the original company**

Preface

Excerpt from a conversation between George F. Walker and Robert Wallace, 15 January 1988.

WALLACE Bazarov reminds me of T.M. Power in *The Power Plays* in that the more he asserts his nihilism, the more he ends up telling everybody he loves them; the more he sets out to destroy the existing order, the more he affects reconciliation amongst the people he meets. After all, his death at the end of the play – the death of a nihilist – would hardly elicit the sympathy it does if he hadn't been able to affect other people with love, even if it was against his wishes.

WALKER I think that's the difficult nature of Bazarov and his journey. At the top of the play, clearly he is unable to talk to the peasant whom he saves from a beating, telling Arkady to deal with his wounds; he can't even say 'you're welcome' to him, the notion being that he can't look the peasants in the eye until they get off their knees. During the play he somehow comes to understand that he has to do that, and that the roots of his nihilism are a profound concern. Unless you reconcile the roots of nihilism with the ways in which your actions affect people, you really are a person out of your time, perhaps out of your planet. If you forget that your work, and all your indignation and your anger, comes from the way people are being treated – the so-called victims – then you can't talk to the victims, and your feeling for them is useless. I watched Bazarov make that journey, took it with him; and I tried to lay in that understanding so that he would undergo more than a mental exercise.

WALLACE The journey that Bazarov undergoes in *Nothing Sacred* seems very similar to the overall journey charted by your plays. If you look at your characters all the way from Ahrun in *Bagdad Saloon*, who is desperate to find or create some sense of self in what is basically a moral and spiritual desert, to those in the East End plays, many of whom are victimized by their marginalized

7

social status, they describe a sort of arc which moves from nothingness – which you might want to talk about as nihilism – to a type of commitment, even action, in the face of social problems.

WALKER I think that's very accurate. You begin with anger and energy; but then you face things – the details of life – and you meet the emptiness that you're afraid of. I think that's true in my work, and it's probably true in my life. It's funny that I'm writing about Bazarov at this time because I read *Fathers and Sons* when I was 17 years old, and I related so strongly to that character then. That I should get around to writing about him when I'm 40, and still relate to him so strongly, is odd because I'm no longer just a son; I'm a father, too, and I have to come to grips with that, to understand that as well.

Introduction

In the spring of 1986, shortly after directing my first George Walker play, *Better Living*, I made a tentative proposal to George for a future project together. Earlier that year I had been unable to obtain production rights to *Wild Honey*, a highly successful adaptation of Chekhov's first play by Englishman Michael Frayne. Remembering George once remarking how much he was drawn to Chekhov's work, I suggested that he write his own version of that play for the Bluma Appel stage. He agreed to give it a try, but after experimenting with several different approaches to the story, got bogged down. What he really wanted to do was write a play about the gamekeeper, but because the character wasn't central to Chekhov's play, George knew he would have to depart too radically from the story. Not wanting to abandon the idea of adapting something Russian, he asked me how I would feel about a play based on Turgenev's *Fathers and Sons*.

What George didn't know was that Turgenev was one of my favourite writers, and *Fathers and Sons* a work I admire so deeply I have given away countless copies to friends over the years. My first response was a mixture of elation and skepticism. The coincidence of our mutual enthusiasm for this novel was almost too good to be true, but I had trouble getting my mind around the idea of turning it into a play. The book is so rich and subtle, so wide-ranging; how could one confine it to a stage without doing Turgenev a terrible disservice? Of course I didn't say that to George, but as intoxicated as I was with the notion, I secretly doubted it could be done. Within a very short time, however, he handed me a remarkable first draft.

Naturally it wasn't the book; yet it *was* Turgenev. Something about the combination of indignation and generosity of feeling, about the vitality and freshness and *irreverence* of Walker's dialogue was profoundly true to the spirit of *Fathers and Sons*. With all the liberties taken (the omission of Bazarov's parents,

Anna's sister, the frogs, and most of the love story; the radical change in Anna's character, the plot tightening, etc.), George had managed to give emotional coherence to what was always implicit in the book, though never as boldly stated, i.e., Turgenev's longing for a better Russia.

At the same time, the academic in me worried about the audacity of putting some of George's words in the mouths of Turgenev's characters. How could we believe we were in nineteenth-century Russia with people saying things like 'I'm in shock,' 'Don't get in a snit,' or 'I'll just wander into the kitchen and pick at things?' I likewise fretted over Anna's bombs, Pavel's nailpolish (not yet invented), over apples being eaten and trays of fruit being proffered in the Russian countryside in May; over Fenichka and Anna greeting people so informally. It wasn't until I was in rehearsal 14 months later that I realized that the play's very contemporary (and Canadian) sensibility was precisely what made it immediate and accessible as opposed to literary and remote. Clearly I hadn't paid attention to George's title.

Going into rehearsals I was anxious, since George had not sent some requested additions we had agreed on. They mostly had to do with the relationship between Anna and Pavel and the plot details surrounding it. It was an area of Turgenev's book where George had taken considerable liberties in the interests of condensing the story. He excused himself by saying that he was afraid of tampering with the play in isolation lest he write something false. If he could see it in rehearsal he would know how to fix it. In fact this proved to be true. George learns so much from his actors, especially when they commit themselves to the text in front of them. When they are uncomfortable with a line that George is not prepared to lose, he will say to them, 'Don't worry, they'll love it in Australia.'

Many of his comments in rehearsal had to do with pace. He encouraged the actors not to get lost in the emotional context of their lines, not to wait for the words to feel 'right' before saying them; to trust in the quick intuitive response that characterizes so much of our conversation in real life. Frequently he would say, 'This is a Canadian comedy, not a Russian tragedy; unless I can hear the play at pace I don't know what I've written.' And it was only when the actors played it for keeps with passion and urgency that George was able to remedy what was wrong or improve on what he already had. I remember him leaping out of his chair one day to give Michael Riley a glorious addition to one of his lines. Arkady has just learned that Bazarov also loves Anna (towards the end of scene four) and is momentarily stunned. 'You love her?' he exclaims. George told him to add, 'All of a sudden you *love* someone? ... And it has to be her!' And on the very afternoon of our opening performance he gave Peter Blais a subtle but deeply funny adjustment to one of Piotr's speeches in the duel scene. Piotr is instructing Bazarov in the etiquette of duelling. The line had read, 'The two gentlemen then raise their weapons and shoot when they wish. That should be the end of it.' George changed the last sentence to 'That should be the end of you ... it.'

True to the spirit of the play, our designer Mary Kerr gave us a set that was as great a challenge to look at as it was to work on. When our carpenters first saw the plans for Mary's raked and rolling floor they shook their heads in dismay. Once they had figured out how to build it, however, their enthusiasm was boundless. They knew they were creating something extraordinary. Alan Laing's music and Lynne Hyde's lighting further enhanced the quality of outrageousness and fun that emanates from the heart of this play. It was one of the rare pleasures of production week to discover how the lighting could best serve and compliment the mischief, the wit and sometimes the sense of wonder in Alan's score.

Early on in the design process Mary had mentioned she was taking her cue from Bazarov's line, 'I look at the world and think of ways of taking it all apart. Starting from scratch ...' One of the wonderful things about *Nothing Sacred* is that it was able to push us all – actors,

11

designers, technicians, and finally, the audience – in that direction. To dismantle and rebuild is feasible in the world of George's play. All of us want and need to believe that life also holds out that possibility.

Bill Glassco
April 1988

Nothing Sacred

Nothing Sacred was first produced by CentreStage Company, in the Bluma Appel Theatre of the St. Lawrence Centre for the Arts, Toronto, 14 January 1988, with the following cast:

BAZAROV, *Robert Bockstael*
ARKADY, *Michael Riley*
NIKOLAI (PETROVICH) KIRSANOV, *David Fox*
PAVEL (PETROVICH) KIRSANOV, *Richard Monette*
FENICHKA, *Beverley Cooper*
ANNA, *Diane D'Aquila*
SITNIKOV, *Ross Manson*
PIOTR, *Peter Blais*
BAILIFF, *Christopher Benson*
GREGOR, *John Dolan*
SERGEI, *Patrick Tierney*

Directed by Bill Glassco
Set and Costumes designed by Mary Kerr
Lighting designed by Lynne Hyde
Music composed by Alan Laing

Persons

YEVGENY (VASSILYICH) BAZAROV, *25*
ARKADY (NIKOLAYEVICH) KIRSANOV, *23*
NIKOLAI (PETROVICH) KIRSANOV, *(Arkady's father), 47*
PAVEL (PETROVICH) KIRSANOV, *(Arkady's uncle), 48*
FENICHKA (NIKOLAEVNA), *19*
ANNA (SERGYEVNA) ODINTSOV, *early 30s*
VIKTOR SITNIKOV, *25*
PIOTR, *a servant, an energetic 80 year old*
BAILIFF
GREGOR, *(a young peasant)*
SERGEI, *(a large peasant)*

The play takes place in Russia, in late spring, 1859. The periphery of the set should be a kind of minimalist landscape. Mostly open fields with the occasional slope. A suggestion of forests. The rest is a bare dark hardwood floor. The various locations in the play must be suggested simply with as few pieces of furniture as possible.

Note
Intermission should be placed between Scenes Four and Five.

Chris Benson (Bailiff), Robert Bockstael (Bazarov), Michael Riley (Arkady) and John Dolan (Gregor)

Prologue

Darkness
Sounds of someone being beaten
Lights
Roadside
A raggedy peasant, GREGOR, *on his knees. His hands held behind his back. Over him stands a* BAILIFF *brandishing a switch*
Behind them, watching with a bemused expression, is ARKADY KIRSANOV, *twenty-three, a pleasant looking young man in a great coat and a student's hat. He is clutching a carpet bag to his chest*

BAILIFF One more for good measure.

GREGOR Whatever pleases the bailiff.

BAILIFF In that case four or five.
[*He hits him*]

GREGOR A little higher please. I think you've opened up a terrible wound in that spot. Feel it. It feels wet and spongy.

BAILIFF Feel it yourself.
[*He hits him again*]

GREGOR That wasn't higher at all. I ... I think I'm gonna go fainting here.

BAILIFF If you pass out it doesn't count. I have to start again after you wake up.

GREGOR Jesus. [*smiles*]

BAILIFF What was that?!
[*He hits him*]

GREGOR Just two more.

BAILIFF Five more.

GREGOR No two more. I've been counting.

BAILIFF You learned to count by stealing things. That reminds me of how much I hate you. Of how much my father hated your father. Another five!
[*He hits him several times*]

GREGOR Please. Keep count out loud. And stop losing control of yourself or this could go on forever. [*He laughs.*] You big dumb pig.
[*The* BAILIFF *yells. Starts to beat him wildly.* GREGOR *moans. Mutters. And occasionally smiles.* BAZAROV

wanders on. He is a tall angular man. Unshaven. Wearing a loose-fitting overcoat. Carrying a suitcase on his shoulder. Staring at something he holds in his free hand. He hears the noise. Looks up. Puts down his suitcase. Puts the object in his hand into his pocket. Takes out a cigar. Walks over and stands beside ARKADY]

BAZAROV Welcome to the new Russia.

ARKADY Can you stop this.

BAZAROV Yes I can. Can you.

ARKADY Is it my place. That man's a bailiff.

BAZAROV And the other one's a thief I suppose.

ARKADY Yes.

BAZAROV Then they're just doing what they've been doing for hundreds of years ... Cigar?

ARKADY No ... But we're against this type of thing, aren't we.

BAZAROV Are we.

ARKADY This is a form of institutional punishment. One man has power given him by the state ... the institution of serfdom.

BAZAROV On the other hand, thieves need to be stopped. Right?

ARKADY Yes. That's what I was thinking while I watched.

BAZAROV You're a good Russian. You can maintain two political points of view at once ... I think he might be killing him. It could be time to take a stand.
[ARKADY *looks at* BAZAROV ... *Then takes a step forward*]

ARKADY Stop. [*He puts down his bag. Then takes a step forward*] Excuse me. [*The* BAILIFF *looks at him*] I've been watching. My opinion is that you've hurt him enough. You should stop now.

BAILIFF Yes sir. But he's ...

ARKADY Yes I know. But unless he's stolen someone's entire estate you've beaten him sufficiently.

BAZAROV [*moving slowly forward*] Unless there is something personal in it. [*to* BAILIFF] Is there something personal in it.

BAILIFF I'm just doing my job. I'm the bailiff for Nikolai Petrovich Kirsanov. His estate is just two kilometres on.

BAZAROV Estate? [*He laughs*]

ARKADY [*to* BAZAROV] Farm! It's really just a farm. [*to* BAILIFF]

Nikolai Petrovich is my father. And I know he'd want
you to stop beating this man right now.

BAZAROV [*to* BAILIFF] Do you often beat people for this young
gentleman's father.

BAILIFF Hardly ever.

BAZAROV So this is a special occasion for you.

BAILIFF Yes ... I mean no. I mean –

BAZAROV And you must get some pleasure from it.

BAILIFF Well I –

BAZAROV There aren't many sources of true pleasure in our
world. Justice is one. Justice completely obtained is a
joyous vibrant thing. But then you know that. You're a
bailiff. But did you know that justice was made to be like
a wheel of fire. It turns. And when it turns, it burns!
[BAZAROV *puts his hand around the* BAILIFF's *neck. He lifts.*
The BAILIFF *is on tip-toes*] I believe there was something
personal in this beating. And if that's the case consider
that this man might have friends. Yes even this piece of
half-eaten garbage might have people who love him and
might want to seek their own kind of justice. Love
comes quickly to the wretched. Sometimes. I'm
beginning to love him myself. I'm beginning to love him
quite a lot.
[*He squeezes. The* BAILIFF *gurgles*]

ARKADY Bazarov.

BAZAROV What!?

ARKADY Let him go.

BAZAROV That's not for you to say. It's for the piece of garbage to
say. [*He looks at* GREGOR] Well?

GREGOR I'm thinking.
[BAZAROV *laughs*]

ARKADY [*to* GREGOR] Please!

BAZAROV Don't pressure him now! He's been pressured quite
enough for one day.

ARKADY His face is turning blue.

BAZAROV [*to* GREGOR] While you're thinking you should be in
possession of all the facts, I'm holding his jugular. He'll
be dead in one minute if you don't say anything.

GREGOR Sir. A minute isn't very long to decide something like this. I mean there's a hatred here which is pretty severe. Him for me. Me for him. You know ... if I had just a bit more time I could –

ARKADY Bazarov. Please. This is ridiculous. It's murder.

BAZAROV It's all right. My friend here and I can take the responsibility. [*to* GREGOR] Can't we.

GREGOR Can we? [BAZAROV *shrugs*] Let him go. [BAZAROV *takes his hand off the* BAILIFF's *neck. The* BAILIFF *doubles up. Wheezing. He drops to his knees*]

ARKADY Thank you.

BAZAROV Thank him. [*points to* GREGOR] Go ahead. [*Pause.* ARKADY *looks puzzled*] Relax my friend. Would I really make you thank a piece of garbage. It was just a passing thought. [BAZAROV *goes to retrieve his suitcase.* ARKADY *goes to* GREGOR. *Helps him up*] The wounds on his back are fairly serious. [*leaving*] Tell him to stay away from those stupid peasant home remedies. Tell him to seek out a chemist for disinfectant. If he can't find one he can visit me at your father's estate.

ARKADY Farm.

GREGOR Thank you.

BAZAROV Tell him it was my pleasure. [BAZAROV *leaves. Puffing mightily on his cigar*]

ARKADY Will you be all right.

GREGOR My mother makes a garlic and fish poultice. We use it all the time.

ARKADY You heard what he said about that.

GREGOR Should I believe him.

ARKADY You should if you're smart. He's a doctor.

BAILIFF [*through his teeth*] Some doctor.

ARKADY Well a student actually. [*picking up his bag*] But brilliant ... yes I'd believe him. [*looks at them both*] If I were you. [ARKADY *leaves*] [*The* BAILIFF *and* GREGOR *remain where they are*] [*Staring at one another*] [GREGOR *laughs*] [*Blackout*]

Scene One

The garden of the Kirsanov house
A couple of benches. A small table. Lilac tree
NIKOLAI KIRSANOV *is pacing. Looking occasionally at his*
pocket watch. He is a rumpled, pleasant looking man in
his mid-forties. Wearing checked trousers and an old
sweater
PIOTR *comes on carrying a tray of fruit*

KIRSANOV Are they here.

PIOTR No.

KIRSANOV What do you suppose is keeping them. Why am I asking
you that. What do you know about it.

PIOTR Actually I do have an opinion.

KIRSANOV Go ahead.

PIOTR The carriage. It could have broken down. Broke down
last week.

KIRSANOV The carriage was repaired.

PIOTR Not well.

KIRSANOV How do you know.

PIOTR I repaired it.

KIRSANOV Are you admitting you did a bad job.

PIOTR I did what I could sir. The front axles were severely
warped. There is no money for replacements.

KIRSANOV Who told you that.

PIOTR Your brother, sir.

KIRSANOV Is this my brother's land.

PIOTR Not to my knowledge, sir.

KIRSANOV Piotr. Stop assuming that all my questions require
answers from you. What's that you're carrying.
[PIOTR *just looks at him*]

PIOTR Is that a question I should answer, sir?

KIRSANOV Is that insolence, Piotr.

PIOTR Fruit!

KIRSANOV What? I see it's fruit. Never mind. What's it for. Never
mind. Take it away. Are we Europeans. Never mind. Take
it away. We don't eat in the garden. We eat at a table
indoors.

21

[ARKADY *enters*]

ARKADY Of course we do. Are we barbarians, Piotr. No don't answer that.

KIRSANOV Here's my son. Look at him. Look at him. A university graduate. Come here. [ARKADY *goes to him. They kiss. The Russian style*] You look well.

ARKADY I am. You look tired.

KIRSANOV Oh? Well I ... No I feel fine. I was worried about you. You should have been here three hours ago.

ARKADY Trouble with the carriage. We left it in town with the driver for repairs.

PIOTR Do you know if the repairs will be expensive, monsieur, sir.

ARKADY I didn't ask. [*to* KIRSANOV] Should I have found out, Father. Before asking the blacksmith to go ahead.

PIOTR Yes.

KIRSANOV No. Of course not. You can leave now Piotr.

ARKADY You're dressing differently, Piotr. I believe you're speaking differently too.

KIRSANOV Like a European. That's your Uncle Pavel's doing. He's remodelling the domestic help. Foolishness.

PIOTR I have an opinion about that, sir.

KIRSANOV I'm sure you do. But a meal is being prepared inside which needs your supervision so you have to leave here now and ... go ... into ... the ... kitchen.
[PIOTR *bows. Starts off.* BAZAROV *comes in. Takes an apple off* PIOTR's *tray as he passes.* PIOTR *bows to* BAZAROV. BAZAROV *smiles. Bows back.* PIOTR *leaves*]

BAZAROV Why does he bow like that. Is he French.

ARKADY Bazarov come here. My father. Father. This is my best friend in the world.
[*They shake hands*]

KIRSANOV Yevgeny Vassilyich, my son has mentioned you often in his letters. It is a pleasure to have you here with us.

BAZAROV I'm just passing through. I'm on vacation and I have to visit my parents. They live not too far from here. Arkady thought you and I should meet.

KIRSANOV Of course we should meet. And you must stay with us for awhile.

Michael Riley (Arkady), Peter Blais (Piotr) and David Fox (Kirsanov)

BAZAROV We'll see.

ARKADY Don't try to convince him, Father. He comes and goes for his own reasons. No one can figure them out.

BAZAROV Why do they try, I wonder. [*bites the apple*] I'm starving. If you don't mind I think I'll wander into the kitchen and pick at things.

KIRSANOV Oh ... You'll do, what? Pick? Oh. Of course. But we'll be eating soon. An enormous meal is being –

BAZAROV I'm hungry now. I try to eat only when I'm hungry. Sleep only when I'm tired. You and your son the young gentleman graduate here have much to discuss. [BAZAROV *goes off*]

KIRSANOV An ... interesting young man.

ARKADY You're thinking he's rude. But he's not. He's just practical. And he's brilliant. He's had an enormous influence on me. Please be good to him.

KIRSANOV In what way has he influenced you.

ARKADY In how to look at things. Institutions. Traditions ... the rest.

KIRSANOV And how is that.

ARKADY Critically.

23

KIRSANOV I see. Are you looking at me critically now.

ARKADY You're not an institution, Father. You're a gentleman farmer. Besides I love you faults and all.

KIRSANOV And I love you friends and all ... [*laughs, grabs him*] Come here. Look at you. I'm so proud.

ARKADY Graduating wasn't difficult. What do I do now.

KIRSANOV Anything you want. [*He holds him at arm's length*] What do you want by the way. [ARKADY *shrugs*] He shrugs. He shrugs. But I know he can do better. He's a university graduate. He can use words.

ARKADY I ... want to change things.

KIRSANOV Arkady, is that your friend talking.

ARKADY We can discuss this later. How is farm life.

KIRSANOV Oh, it's ... No I won't lie to you. Well perhaps a little. [*laughs*] No. Difficult. The new laws. Nobody is sure. I have as you know one of the most liberal practices anywhere. I have turned from serfdom to tenant farming. Some of the ... working tenants ... work. Some ... steal. I haven't a great deal of experience in management so ...

[FENICHKA *comes on. A baby wrapped in a blanket in her arms*]

FENICHKA Oh. Please excuse me. We ... I ... was just getting some ... air. [*She leaves*]

ARKADY Was that your young housekeeper.

KIRSANOV Fenichka. Yes. Fenichka has –

ARKADY A baby.

KIRSANOV Yes! What? Yes. A baby. She has a baby. But –

ARKADY No husband?

KIRSANOV What? No. No she has no ...

ARKADY Husband?

KIRSANOV But that's a long story. [*looks at his watch*] I think I have something to do now, if I could just remember what it is ... Perhaps later this evening we could sit down and talk about all these things. Your friend. My farm. Fenichka's ... husband. Yes. Now I remember. I have to go. I'm sorry. A matter with my bailiff. [KIRSANOV *starts off*]

ARKADY Oh Father. About your bailiff.

KIRSANOV Yes?

ARKADY Perhaps we can discuss him later as well.

KIRSANOV Certainly. Put him on the list. We'll talk about
everything. I promise. [*looks at his watch*] Your Uncle
Pavel should be getting up soon.

ARKADY He's still taking long naps?

KIRSANOV Longer. Much longer.
[*He leaves*]
[ARKADY *looks around. Sits*]
[FENICHKA *comes back on. Without the baby*]

ARKADY [*stands*] Hello.

FENICHKA Hello.

ARKADY I'm Arkady. We met briefly last year.

FENICHKA Yes. Hello ...

ARKADY Hello.

FENICHKA I believe I was rude earlier. I came to apologize. And to
welcome you back to your home properly.

ARKADY That's not necessary.

FENICHKA Oh. Yes it is. I'm sorry. And welcome. I mean I'm very
pleased that you are here with your father. He needs
you desperately. No I shouldn't have said that.
[*She leaves. Shaking her head. Talking to herself.
Bumping into* UNCLE PAVEL *on his way on. He is reading a
small book of poetry.* PAVEL *is a healthy looking man.
Close cropped hair. Clean shaven. Wearing dark suit of
English cut. Opal cufflinks. Pink nail polish*]

FENICHKA [*a gentle scream*] Ohh. It's you. Please excuse me.

PAVEL No it is you who would direct an honour my way by
allowing me to apologize.

FENICHKA Pardon?

PAVEL The fault was all mine.

FENICHKA I hear a baby screaming. [*She runs off*]

PAVEL I hear nothing.

ARKADY Neither do I.

PAVEL [*turns*] Ah! You're here. Good. Let's shake hands.
[*They do*] You are a splendid young man. I always said
so. You have your father's good heart and if you worked
at it you could have my good style.

ARKADY No one has your style, Uncle.

PAVEL Oh there are two or three Englishmen, and a German
baron who do, but otherwise you are quite correct. Let's

hug! [*They do.* PAVEL *wipes away a tear*] Have you seen your father.

ARKADY Yes. He had to run off. Some sort of urgent business.

PAVEL Poor man. He is always running off. Stumbling back. Falling into bed exhausted. For the most part, his life is a disaster. Poor lovely man ... Where's my fruit ... He does have one small consolation. You just saw her?

ARKADY Fenichka? But she's —

PAVEL A child? A housekeeper? A semi-literate? I thought your generation was above those judgements.

ARKADY We are. I mean I wasn't ... I was just ... Why didn't he introduce us properly. Explain.

PAVEL He's in love. He behaves stupidly around her. Besides, what should he explain to you.

ARKADY The baby.

PAVEL Frightened are you, by the notion that you're no longer the only heir?

ARKADY That never entered my mind, honestly.

PAVEL Ask him about the baby yourself. I'm saying nothing about it. So tell me about your future. Law? The military? The civil service. I suggest, of course, the military. Like your grandfather, the great general. Like me the not so great captain.

ARKADY Never the military. It's corrupt from top to bottom.

PAVEL Really. How did you discover that.

ARKADY It's a well known fact.

PAVEL Really. I must be out of touch. Perhaps I've been in the country too long.

ARKADY I realize you feel a certain loyalty to the army.

PAVEL Not true. But I do find it necessary from time to time to ask your generation to be more specific with its criticisms. [BAZAROV *comes on. Munching on a chicken leg.* PAVEL *turns to him abruptly*] You. The stables are in the rear. Deliver whatever it is you have brought. Then feel free to leave. Thank you very much.
[ARKADY *is in shock, until* BAZAROV *laughs*]

ARKADY Uncle. I'm sorry. This is my dear friend. Bazarov.
[PAVEL *looks at them both*]

PAVEL I am deeply shamed.
[*He bows formally*]

BAZAROV So am I.
[*He bows formally*]
PAVEL I beg your pardon.
BAZAROV To allow my dress to deteriorate to a point where a
gentleman such as yourself could make such a foolish
mistake. Please accept my apology.
PAVEL Well the truth is, I believe I owe you the apology.
BAZAROV Then let's just say we're both fools and shake hands.
PAVEL Well ... Yes. Of course.
[PAVEL *extends his hand.* BAZAROV *throws away his chicken
leg. Extends a hand. They shake.* BAZAROV *raises* PAVEL's
hand to look at it]
BAZAROV Do you have a fungus infection under your fingernails?
PAVEL No.
BAZAROV So the pink nail polish is just decoration.
[PAVEL *withdraws his hand*]
PAVEL You find it ... distasteful?
BAZAROV No. Only superfluous.
ARKADY My uncle is well-known in Moscow and Petersburg as a
leader in fashion.
PAVEL But I'm sure your friend finds fashion superfluous. [*to*
BAZAROV] Correct?
BAZAROV Correct.
PAVEL Then we should change the subject immediately.
BAZAROV In a moment, if you don't mind. Is that an English suit.
PAVEL English cut. Russian cloth.
BAZAROV So you are leading us into the fashion of the English.
PAVEL At this moment in our history we could learn much
from the English. The aristocracy in particular.
BAZAROV What exactly.
ARKADY Yes, Uncle. What?
PAVEL The English aristocracy never yield one iota of their
rights. And for that reason they respect the rights of
others. They demand the fulfilment of obligations due to
them, and therefore they fulfil their own obligations to
others.
BAZAROV I see we have changed the subject successfully. We're
now talking about politics.
ARKADY Do you resent the new rights for the serfs, Uncle. You've
always been so kind to them, I thought.

BAZAROV My young friend here still has a weak spot in his heart. Excuse me while I cut it out. [*to* ARKADY] What in God's name has kindness to do with justice!? What has attitude of any kind to do with what is natural. Or what is the law!?

ARKADY I was merely being kind to my uncle.

PAVEL He's always been a kind boy. Perhaps you didn't know that. Perhaps in Petersburg he pretended not to be kind.

BAZAROV No he was kind in Petersburg. To people who needed or deserved his kindness.

PAVEL I think we should stop now. If one gets off on the wrong foot it is necessary to pause before getting back into step. That is perhaps the only useful thing the army taught me. That, and how to shoot with deadly accuracy of course. So I'll retire now and we'll meet later for dinner, when I am less enervated and you are perhaps –

BAZAROV Better dressed?

PAVEL Better tempered.

[PAVEL *starts to bow. Stops himself. Shrugs. Leaves*]

ARKADY Let me explain about my uncle.

BAZAROV Your uncle is perfectly clear to me.

ARKADY You're judging just what you see.

BAZAROV When I see the rest I'll judge the rest. If you are going to tell me he's got a good soul that's not fair. You know I don't understand what that word means.

ARKADY He's had a difficult life.

BAZAROV If you continue to say things like that to me one day I might bite your lips off. He's one of the many sorts of country gentry. What could there be in his past to possibly justify his ridiculous clothes and manners.

ARKADY Love. A great love that wasn't returned.

BAZAROV So he played his cards with a woman and he lost. And that turned him into a fop.

ARKADY He ... I believe he merely took comfort in what was expected of him. What he had some chance at being successful at.

BAZAROV You have a poet's understanding of life.

ARKADY There is no need to be insulting.

BAZAROV Harden yourself. Or you won't be any use in our kind of work.

28

ARKADY So you have decided on a course of action.

BAZAROV No secret there. I'm going to study medicine and
natural science and chemistry and physics as you know.
You are going to do ... well if you ever get around to
choosing a profession, I'm sure you'll be successful at ...
whatever it is.

ARKADY Yes. Yes. But what else.

BAZAROV Ah. You mean actually. Truly. What subversive things
will we be doing at night.

ARKADY I suppose I mean that ... in a way. Yes what subversive
things *will* we be doing at night.
[BAZAROV *puts his hand on* ARKADY's *chest*]

BAZAROV Staying alert. [BAZAROV *puts his foot behind* ARKADY's *feet.
Pushes.* ARKADY *falls*] You should start practising
immediately, my young friend. [BAZAROV *starts off*]

ARKADY Why are you always calling me your young friend. We're
practically the same age.
[BAZAROV *stops*]

BAZAROV Time means very little. Experience not much more. The
important thing is perception. You look at the world and
still perceive some kind of future for it with one thing
leading to another with a few humane modifications
along the way. I look at the world and think of ways of
taking it all apart. Starting again from scratch ... But of
course you know that ... I think you just like to find new
ways of making me say it again ...
[*He leaves*]

ARKADY Yes ... Until I understand what he actually means by it ...
Chemistry ... Physics ... Bombs. Yes ... Or maybe ... No.
Bombs. He's going to blow things up. Churches.
Government buildings. Military headquarters. I couldn't
... Well I could ... yes I could do that too ... If there was
no other way ... Banks ... Luxury hotels ... Libraries ... [*He
looks around*] Farms?
[*Blackout*]

Scene Two

Begin in darkness
The sound of several people arguing loudly
Lights up
*The Kirsanov drawing room. A small supper table. The
meal is over.* KIRSANOV, ARKADY, BAZAROV, *and* FENICHKA *are
seated.* PAVEL *is pacing a few feet away*
PIOTR *is standing upstage of them. Hands behind his back.
Expressionless*

PAVEL All right! All right, please!! Please let me speak.

ARKADY [*stands*] I think you're wrong. Simply wrong!

KIRSANOV A little respect! Please the supper is ruined!

FENICHKA I hear the baby.

KIRSANOV You see you've woken the baby!

PAVEL To hell with the baby!

KIRSANOV Pavel!

PAVEL Let me speak!

ARKADY I was speaking! You interrupted!

PAVEL Well let me interrupt then! Please!

FENICHKA Please! I should go to the baby!

KIRSANOV The baby has a nurse doesn't he!

FENICHKA Why are you yelling at me Nikolai.

KIRSANOV Oh. I'm sorry. [*to the others*] You see. I'm yelling at her!

ARKADY I was simply trying to say that respect is not something
you take for granted!

PAVEL Principles! I want to talk about principles.

ARKADY Yes there's the problem, Uncle. You think I don't respect
your principles. What I actually said was that your
principles are linked to certain traditions –

PAVEL If you ignore tradition you ignore what we are made of.
You don't know the Russian people. They hold tradition
sacred. How can you work for them if you don't know
them. But that's not my point. Please please I beg you let
me make my point!! [BAZAROV *has just finished eating*]

BAZAROV Cigar?

KIRSANOV / PAVEL / ARKADY No!

BAZAROV Let him make his point, Arkady. All this shouting is
upsetting this young woman.
[BAZAROV *lights a cigar*]

FENICHKA No I'm all right. Thank you. But I'm worried –

KIRSANOV Honestly, Fenichka. The baby will survive without you for an evening. You should be here with us.

ARKADY I think so too. In fact, I'm the one who insisted that you dine with us.

KIRSANOV There. You see?

FENICHKA [*to* ARKADY] I'm grateful, believe me.

BAZAROV You need his permission to eat, do you.

ARKADY Please Bazarov. Of course not. What she meant – What I meant –

PAVEL What he meant was, he doesn't care about your station in life one way or the other, Fenichka. He loves his father. If his father is happy, he's happy.

BAZAROV What is all this about.

KIRSANOV Pavel.

PAVEL Oh for God's sake. Can't we air this thing.

KIRSANOV [*to* BAZAROV] A family matter.

BAZAROV I'll leave.

KIRSANOV No please. I believe we were talking about principles.

PAVEL That's the ticket! Now to our young friends here, I am simply an empty poseur.

ARKADY Uncle.

PAVEL I know you love me. But we're not speaking of love. We're speaking of beliefs. Of dignity.

BAZAROV No. Principles, remember?

PAVEL I remember better than you. We were eating a few moments ago. You asked me to explain my earlier comments about the English aristocracy. I explained that what I meant by that was that – simply put – if you don't respect yourself you cannot respect others.

ARKADY Yes. And I said – no, Bazarov said that it didn't matter if you respected yourself or not – that it would have the same impact on the population at large. Namely – none –

PAVEL Yes. Because we of the aristocracy are the men of folded arms, aren't we. Big gaudy do-nothings.

ARKADY But what I said after that was –

PAVEL A simple addendum to what your friend had already said. Be still Arkady. My quarrel is with the man in black here.

Beverley Cooper (Fenichka), Robert Bockstael (Bazarov) and David Fox (Kirsanov)

BAZAROV You don't like my clothes. I'm sorry. It's the closest I have to something decent to eat in. Besides it was the only thing that was clean.

PAVEL It is the uniform of a nihilist.

[*Pause*]

KIRSANOV A what.

ARKADY Nihilist. It comes from the Latin. Nihil. It means –

PAVEL Nothing.

ARKADY Exactly. [*to* KIRSANOV] The word is now used in the cities mostly to describe a kind of man. A man who recognizes nothing.

PAVEL Or respects nothing.

ARKADY A man who ... looks at everything critically. Takes no principles for granted.

PAVEL Principles! What do you know –

ARKADY Please I was going to say that we don't recognize authority and to be 'principled' as you say –

KIRSANOV You said 'we', son. Are you a what's-it-called too.

ARKADY Nihilist. Well ... Yes.

PAVEL Doctrine. They think they've invented it. The philosophy of disrespect has been here before. It always proves to be bankrupt.

32

BAZAROV If I may –

PAVEL Yes.

BAZAROV The baby *is* crying. And coughing too.

FENICHKA [*to* KIRSANOV] Please let me go to him.

KIRSANOV Certainly.

BAZAROV I might be of help.

FENICHKA No that's not necessary.

BAZAROV I know some medicine.

KIRSANOV Then please go with her.

[BAZAROV *stands*]

FENICHKA Excuse me.

[*She leaves*]

BAZAROV Fine dinner. Especially the soup. Very much like my mother makes. And she is an excellent cook.

PAVEL We'll continue this later.

BAZAROV I don't think so. I think you enjoy debating too much for my taste.

PAVEL Well if there's a reason I do –

BAZAROV I believe you should state your case if you're asked, then leave it. Thoughts aren't like laundry. They don't need to be hung out to dry.

[KIRSANOV *is gesturing* PAVEL *to sit down*]

PAVEL But ... but I would ... Please humour an old ... older man. I would simply like to know what you are planning to do after you have torn everything down.

BAZAROV Seriously?

PAVEL Of course!

BAZAROV Nothing.

PAVEL What?

[BAZAROV *goes to* PAVEL]

BAZAROV I'll do nothing. The tearing down is sufficient. In fact an entire life's work. The next generation can do the building. As for your earlier comments. Principles mean nothing to me. Neither as an idea nor a word. Other words. Aristocratism, liberalism, progress. Just empty words. Useless words. And foreign words to boot. I simply base my conduct on what is useful ... Oh a few years ago we 'young people' were saying that our officials took bribes, that we had no roads, no trade, no impartial courts of justice –

PAVEL   Of course, I understand those accusations. In fact, I
agree with many of your criticisms but –

BAZAROV   *Then* we realized that just to keep on talking about our
social diseases was a waste of time, and merely led to a
trivial doctrinaire attitude. We saw that our clever men,
our so-called progressives and reformers never
accomplished anything, that we were concerning
ourselves with a lot of nonsense, discussing art, abstract
creative work, parliamentarianism, the law and the devil
knows what, while all the while the real question was
getting daily bread to eat, stopping the vulgar
superstitions of our church, preventing our fledgling
industries from coming to grief because of the crooks
who run them, and realizing that the government's so-
called emancipation of the serfs will do us no good
because the serfs are so without pride that they spend
most of their time robbing each other and drinking
themselves into oblivion.

PAVEL   And so knowing all this convinced you to become a
nihilist. In effect, to do nothing.

[BAZAROV *stiffens. Then smiles crookedly. Shakes his
head*]

BAZAROV   Well at least nothing I could describe to you. Or nothing
you could understand. [*He leaves*]

PAVEL   Arrogant arrogant man!

[*He pounds the table*]

PAVEL   Arrogant! [*points at* KIRSANOV] And if I were you I'd think
twice about letting a man who respects nothing, fears
nothing, feels nothing, be alone with that young girl!
[*starts off. Stops*] That's what I say.

[PAVEL *leaves*]

[*Pause*]

[KIRSANOV *and* ARKADY *look at each other. Both smiling
weakly*]

KIRSANOV   Some of what he said I agree with.

ARKADY   Who.

KIRSANOV   Bazarov. The superstitions in our culture do a great deal
of damage ... Almost everything else he said made me
sad. I'm not at all like your Uncle Pavel. Not so firmly
rooted in the past. Nevertheless ... Actually I thought I

saw a look of sadness on your face when your friend
was speaking at one point.

ARKADY Maybe you did. Maybe I wasn't thinking about what
Bazarov was saying though. I was probably thinking
about you, Papa.

KIRSANOV You've looked around the farm. Yes I know things don't
look so good. When I moved back here three years ago I
had such high hopes. But I have to tell you Arkasha that
in spite of the unpaid bills, the workers who hate me for
not paying them enough, the workers who steal, my
bailiff who is a drunk and a bully and who scares me a
little – I'm happy. No well not exactly. Yes yes I have to
be honest, I'm a bit happy.

ARKADY Well I won't assume you're happy at being a total failure
as a farmer and a businessman. I'll have to guess there's
some other reason.

KIRSANOV Fenichka.

[KIRSANOV *looks at* PIOTR. PIOTR *nods. Turns around so that
his back is to them*]

ARKADY Fenichka. And her baby.

KIRSANOV My baby.

ARKADY My brother.

KIRSANOV Your brother. Yes. You see I hope you ... Well you know
what I hope ... You see, Fenichka's mother died. You
knew that?

ARKADY No.

KIRSANOV Oh. But you know it was her mother who I hired to be
my housekeeper. Naturally she brought Fenichka to live
here with her.

ARKADY Naturally. Certainly.

KIRSANOV When her mother died ... You see Fenichka knew the
house by then. How to keep it ordered ... But that's not
... When her mother died she was alone. I felt a kind of
sympathy ... at first. She's ... well, you can tell, a gentle
person. The sympathy became ... became ...

ARKADY I should be making this easier for you. But I –

KIRSANOV You don't approve.

ARKADY Oh no. It's not that. I just want you to tell me in your
own way. You must have some reason for not having
told me before.

KIRSANOV In a letter? No I couldn't. You see ... I loved your mother. You know that. We don't have to discuss your mother. This is ...

ARKADY You should marry her, Papa.

KIRSANOV I love her.

ARKADY The baby should have your name.

KIRSANOV And yours.

ARKADY Yes.

KIRSANOV That's all right with you?

ARKADY You thought it wouldn't be?

KIRSANOV Well I didn't presume. No that's not the truth. It's not about you. You see, I try to put a foot in the right direction but the other foot won't move with it. I'm afraid there's still something from the old world in me.

ARKADY If you make love to a housekeeper's daughter ... If you love a housekeeper's daughter ... If you're ... a bit happy with her now you'll be happy if you're married to her.

KIRSANOV Marriage is ... it becomes ... a mixture of personal histories. How can you tell if the mixture ...
[ARKADY *gets up. Goes behind his father. Puts his arms around his neck*]

ARKADY You're a good man. You'll do the right thing.

KIRSANOV Perhaps. But how would she feel about being in my world. I don't know how she feels even now. I don't think so but it's possible she only took me ... I mean she could have been afraid of losing her place in the house. What am I saying.

ARKADY She loves you. Believe me. Everybody loves you.

KIRSANOV [*sighs*] Just as long as you love me.
[BAZAROV *comes on*]

KIRSANOV Is the baby all right.

BAZAROV Yes.

KIRSANOV Nothing to be concerned about?

BAZAROV A chill maybe. I left him slurping happily at his mother's breast.

KIRSANOV She nursed the baby in front of you?

BAZAROV That's the way they do things in the country Nikolai Petrovich. She's a very fine young woman. Healthy. Intelligent. Direct.

KIRSANOV Direct?

BAZAROV She opened up. We had a good little talk. Wouldn't tell me who the father was though. I assume it is you sir. I couldn't stomach the idea of it being your brother.

KIRSANOV Excuse me!? Yes ... [*awkwardly*] Excuse me.
[*He leaves*]

ARKADY That was grotesque! Grotesque and heartless!

BAZAROV Oh let's strip the veneer from these gentle country barons, my friend. Let's clear the air and see where we really are. Or aren't you up to it.

ARKADY So that was a test for my sake.

BAZAROV Or maybe mine. Who knows. Or maybe I just spoke the truth. As simple as that.
[*A commotion*]
[PIOTR *faces out again*]
[*The* BAILIFF *staggers on. Followed by* KIRSANOV, *trying to restrain him. The* BAILIFF *is drunk. Carrying a large board*]

KIRSANOV What are you doing here? Who do you think you are brushing past me like that.
[*The* BAILIFF *shakes* KIRSANOV'*s arm off*]

BAILIFF Out of my way.

KIRSANOV But I own this farm. I'm the owner. I can't believe you're talking to me this way.

BAILIFF Am I a human being. Are you a human being. Can't human beings talk.

KIRSANOV Of course. But not like this! I mean you shouldn't be here. And that's final!
[KIRSANOV *grabs the* BAILIFF'*s arm again. The* BAILIFF *shakes him off.* KIRSANOV *falls.* ARKADY *goes to help him up*]

BAILIFF Get off me! I've got business here all right. [*to* BAZAROV] So you tricked me before. But I don't forget. I never forget. I checked around. You're nothing special. You're not an official person. I can fix you all right. And nothing happens.

BAZAROV Officially, you mean.

BAILIFF You tricked me. I wasn't ready for ya. [*He advances*] I'm ready now.
[*He swings the board at* BAZAROV]
[BAZAROV *ducks under the board. Throws the* BAILIFF

forward. The BAILIFF *falls on his face.* BAZAROV *grabs a plate from the table. The* BAILIFF *is on his knees now.* BAZAROV *breaks the plate across the back of the* BAILIFF'S *head. The* BAILIFF *falls unconscious*]

PIOTR That plate was over two hundred years old!

KIRSANOV Bazarov!

ARKADY Bazarov.

BAZAROV [*to* ARKADY] Oh I forgot. We've got an invitation to stay with a mutual friend in town. His father owns a hotel. I think it was time we were moving on anyway.
[*Blackout*]

Scene Three

The sitting room of a hotel suite
A couch, a chair. A large floral arrangement
BAZAROV, ARKADY, *and* SITNIKOV *are drinking champagne.*
BAZAROV *is smoking a cigar. Chuckling at* SITNIKOV.
Throwing back glass after glass. Lounging on the couch.
ARKADY *is reading a book. Sipping.* SITNIKOV *is on his feet*
telling a story which he finds particularly funny. He is a
short man. He wears a Slavic jacket. And European
trousers. He has a strange laugh which he accomplishes
by sucking in air and somehow producing an extended
'ee' sound

SITNIKOV   Eeeeeee. But the governor says to my father, 'This is my province, if you want to do business here you have to make me feel that you like me.' So ... my father kissed him. Eeeeee. That's funny. I know that's funny. But this is funnier. My father meant it. He told me later that he *did* like the governor, that he thought, all in all, he was a pleasant man. So he ... eeeee, kissed him with genuine warmth. Needless to say the governor looked on my father from that moment on as a potentially unstable business partner and my father was not allowed to establish the system of trade he wanted, so he sought my advice. 'Buy a hotel' I said ... eeeeeee. I was joking you see. It was the first thing that came into my head. So he did ... eeeeeee. And here we are. Drinking his champagne. Eeeeeeee.
[BAZAROV *sits up suddenly*]

BAZAROV   Viktor! If the point of that amazingly long and only mildly amusing story was merely to demonstrate that your father is a fool, I will ... rip out your tonsils.
[SITNIKOV *sobers immediately*]

SITNIKOV   Yes. And you'd be quite right too. No of course the point of the story is ... is ... this – even though good things can sometimes come from bad practices we must always be attempting to turn those good things back –

BAZAROV   Into a joke.

SITNIKOV   Well no ... But Yevgeny you used to enjoy a good joke.

BAZAROV   I still do.

39

SITNIKOV I see but now is not the time. I see. We are graduates now. Yes. The time now and the time ahead is serious business. If that's what you say, I am your disciple and that is how I shall start behaving immediately.

BAZAROV Good. Here is the first piece of serious business I wish you to undertake. Go get more champagne.

SITNIKOV Of course. [*starts off. Stops. Points at* BAZAROV] Eeeeee. You tricked me.

BAZAROV Eeeeeee. A little.

SITNIKOV Never mind. I am your disciple truly. I don't mind.
[*He leaves*]
[BAZAROV *practices* SITNIKOV's *laugh*]

ARKADY [*still reading*] When did he become your disciple.

BAZAROV You'd have to say it was a gradual process. Almost imperceptible. Or else I would have put a stop to it.

ARKADY Would you.

BAZAROV There is not much to be gained by having imbeciles as disciples.

ARKADY But you don't object to the notion of having disciples as a rule.

BAZAROV What are you reading.

ARKADY Nothing you'd find very interesting.
[BAZAROV *sits up. Grabs the book*]

BAZAROV A manual on agricultural management. A German manual?

ARKADY I'm sorry but they happen to be the foremost experts on the subject. I'm looking for ways of advising my father.

BAZAROV Really! [*He throws the book back*] I liked your father more or less.

ARKADY How generous of you to say so.

BAZAROV Now don't get in a snit. I was being honest. I found him to be intelligent and kind. I wasn't too happy about the way he's keeping that girl – his young flame – flickering in the corner.

ARKADY You don't understand that. So we shouldn't talk about it. My father has some problems regarding his feelings. I think that's quite common in men his age.

BAZAROV Oh come now. His problems there are about class. His class. Her class. The 'indecent' distance between the two. You know that as well as I. And if you're going to be

blind stupid, sentimental and obstinate about it, then
you're right we shouldn't talk!
[ARKADY *stands*]

ARKADY I've changed my mind. I think this is politically
important. One strong piece of rope ... together is
stronger than a bunch of smaller ropes tied ... together.

BAZAROV The poet is struggling to find his metaphor here. Be
careful.

ARKADY If you take a generation ... or if a generation is taken and
... or not taken, if you don't attempt to heal the ... [*He
sits*]

BAZAROV Simply please. Just say it.

ARKADY It's better ... to educate these old fellows and thereby
enlist their help for the future.

BAZAROV No time. Not enough energy. Much more difficult than
you could imagine. Basically unnecessary.

ARKADY Take my father and my uncle as examples –
[BAZAROV *stands*]

BAZAROV Your uncle is absurd. He embodies much of what is
wrong with this country. He lusts after foreign
influences. He wears clothes that allow him to pretend
he is actually living somewhere else. He uses make-up
to contour his broad Russian face into something like an
English ferret. He can't look simple peasants in the eye
because they terrify him. Not because of what they
might do to him someday but because of what they are.
And what they are is Russian! Russian. For better or
worse! Russian! ... [*He takes a drink*] As for your father.
The merciful thing is to let him alone. Let him die as he
lived. Don't go trying to fill his head with bright new
ideas. Unless you want him to stumble to his grave in
chaos.
[*They are looking at one another*]
[SITNIKOV *comes on. Three bottles of champagne*]

SITNIKOV Mission accomplished.
[*They ignore him*]

ARKADY But what about love.

BAZAROV What about it.

ARKADY Are you against love.

BAZAROV What kind of a question is that.

Michael Riley (Arkady), Ross Manson (Viktor) and Robert Bockstael (Bazarov)

ARKADY We've never really talked about it before. Seeing my father again, I realize how much I love him.

BAZAROV I love my father as well. So?

ARKADY So what is it? Love. Is it a kind of social necessity under certain circumstances. In a family for example. Or something else.

BAZAROV Something else, probably. Since your first definition doesn't make any sense.

SITNIKOV I'd have to agree with that.

ARKADY Shut up.

SITNIKOV You can't tell me to shut up.

BAZAROV Can I tell you to shut up, Viktor.

ARKADY Would it be a kind of elemental human characteristic for example. Something untouchable. Incomprehensible?

BAZAROV Everything is comprehensible. You take the conditions. And measure them against the facts.

ARKADY Like a science.

BAZAROV Listen friend. If you're searching for some rationale for excusing certain kinds of behaviour you don't need my help. There are hundreds of novels, thousands of poems, in fact an entire world of art that will allow you to do that. You'll probably turn to them eventually. You might as well do it now.

ARKADY You don't believe I have the stomach for hard choices, do you.

BAZAROV This is the last summer vacation Arkady. Use it. I'm using it. Drink champagne. I'm drinking champagne. Spend time with fools. [*Puts his arm around* SITNIKOV] I'm spending time with fools. Be as natural as you want. Autumn comes soon enough. When the leaves change you can change with them if you decide. Come on. That's as close to poetry as you'll ever get from me. And I did it just for you.
[*He hugs* ARKADY]

SITNIKOV Do you truly think I'm a fool Yevgeny. I know you use humour as a cruel weapon. To cut to the truth. But ... I can't stay here in the room with you if that is your true opinion of me. I have a little pride, you know.

BAZAROV Then it's a precious commodity. I suggest you save it by

43

finding the door. [SITNIKOV *starts off*] Viktor. [SITNIKOV *stops*]

SITNIKOV Yes Yevgeny.

BAZAROV Eeeeeee. [*He smiles*]

SITNIKOV Another trick. Eeeeeee. God bless you. If he existed, of course. [SITNIKOV *rushes to them. Awkwardly hugs them both*] Three friends embrace. They drink they think they quarrel. But eventually they embrace. It's summer. Let things occur they say. Autumn will come. Then we'll see if the world's safe. Eeeeeeeee.

[*Pause*]

[ANNA ODINTSOV *comes on. She is about thirty. Tall, wealthy, sparking ironic expression*]

[*They don't see her*]

[SERGEI *comes on carrying two suitcases. Stands beside her*]

ANNA Gentlemen. [*They turn*] Young gentlemen. Excuse me. [*They look at her. They are impressed. They look at each other.* SITNIKOV *breaks away first*] You are in my room.

SITNIKOV What was that.

ANNA This room. The bedrooms. The entire suite ... is mine.

SITNIKOV Madame Odintsov?

ANNA Correct.

SITNIKOV No it wasn't a question. I know your name of course. Let me explain.

BAZAROV Yes please let him explain. It's bound to be a treat to watch.

SITNIKOV I am Viktor Sitnikov. We have met on several occasions.

ANNA Strange. I have no recollection of you.

SITNIKOV No? Well no. Why should you. Who am I.

ANNA Very well. Who are you.

BAZAROV Continue Viktor. No disappointment so far.

SITNIKOV My father owns this hotel.

ANNA Is that an important fact.

SITNIKOV Well no. Not in itself. How do you mean. I'm not a status seeker.

BAZAROV Ouch. [*to* ARKADY] The man is a comic genius.

ANNA Does the fact that your father owns the hotel somehow give you permission to occupy my rooms when I'm not here.

SITNIKOV Good heavens. Do you think I do this on a regular basis.

BAZAROV Good boy Viktor. Go blindly to the offensive.

SITNIKOV Please, Bazarov.

SERGEI Do you want me to throw them out ma'am.

ANNA Yes after they've explained what they're doing here you can throw them out.

SITNIKOV Who is that. Who are you. You're not one of our porters.

ANNA Sergei works for me.

BAZAROV A bodyguard. [*to* ARKADY] Quite a body too.

SERGEI She heard that. Didn't you, ma'am.

ANNA No.

BAZAROV Do you want me to repeat it.

SITNIKOV Oh dear. Things are getting worse. Listen. [*He begins to gather the glasses and empty bottles*] Why don't we just leave and I'll explain later. It's a small misunderstanding. Perhaps I misread the calendar.

BAZAROV I'm staying.

SITNIKOV Bazarov.

BAZAROV No I'm definitely staying. There's something about this woman that attracts me.

SERGEI Do you want me to hit him hard, ma'am.

ANNA No. Perhaps later I'll let you hit him hard. In the meantime please take my luggage into the bedroom.

SERGEI Whatever you say.

[*He goes*]

ANNA [*to* SITNIKOV] You may leave now.

SITNIKOV Of course. Come on friends.

ANNA Just you. This rude one here and his silent friend can stay awhile ... if they wish.

ARKADY Oh no that –

BAZAROV Shush.

[ANNA *stares at* SITNIKOV]

[*He leaves*]

[ANNA *and* BAZAROV *stare at one another*]

[BAZAROV *walks to her slowly. Puts his hand on her cheek. Kisses her. Embraces her. She returns the embrace. The kiss becomes passionate*]

[ARKADY *is frozen. His eyes wide*]

[*Still kissing* ANNA, BAZAROV *puts out a hand to* ARKADY]

[ARKADY's *eyes get even wider. He backs off.* BAZAROV

45

*Michael Riley (Arkady), Robert Bockstael (Bazarov) and Diane
D'Aquila (Anna)*

snaps his fingers. ARKADY *slowly moves in. Takes*
BAZAROV's *hand*]
[BAZAROV *steps back. Puts* ARKADY's *hand in* ANNA's *hand*]
Arkady Nikolayevich Kirsanov please meet my old friend
Anna Sergyevna Odintsov.
[ANNA *gives a gentle laugh*]

ANNA   I've heard so much about you, Arkady.

ARKADY   You ... You're, you're his –

ANNA   His friend the widow. The one with the reputation.

ARKADY   No. I meant I've heard so much about you as well.
Everything except your name ... no not everything ... I
mean –

BAZAROV   Please Arkady you're beginning to sound like Viktor. [*to*
ANNA] Speaking of Viktor, you were very cruel to him
Anna.

ANNA   I got the distinct impression you wanted me to be even
crueler.

BAZAROV   I don't know what it is about him that stirs malice in
me. I'd like to be philosophical and think it's his manner
or his attitude, but I think it's actually his face.

ARKADY   You planned this?

BAZAROV   Haphazardly. When Viktor suggested we make ourselves

46

comfortable somewhere in the hotel I bribed a porter
into delivering us here. Then I bribed him to tell Viktor
that Anna wasn't expected for a week. The rest I left to
Madame Odintsov's wonderful sense of occasion.

ARKADY I'll go find Viktor. He could be slitting his wrists.

ANNA Over something so small.

ARKADY Not that you found him here. But that he wasn't allowed
to stay. Like we were.

BAZAROV Yes. His manhood has been questioned. He won't
actually understand that. But he'll be deeply depressed
nonetheless. My fault ... I'll go fix it. You two get
acquainted.
[BAZAROV *leaves*]

ANNA Please sit.

ARKADY May I help you with your cloak.

ANNA Thank you.
[*He does*]
[SERGEI *comes on*]

SERGEI That's done, ma'am.

ANNA Thank you, Sergei.

SERGEI I'm new at this remember, ma'am. What should I do
now. Should I prepare your bath? Polish furniture?

ANNA I prepare my own bath Sergei. That's not part of your
job. What I wish you to do is make a bed of sorts for
yourself outside my door.

SERGEI And stay there? And guard it?

ANNA Yes.

SERGEI Yes. I can do that ... No problem.
[*He leaves*]

ARKADY So he is a body guard then?

ANNA Yes.

ARKADY But why –

ANNA Oh the usual reasons.

ARKADY Sergei. Just ... Sergei?

ANNA We don't use his other name. Sheep-in-a-ditch-in-love
or something like that. Hideous. [*She sits*] Please sit
down. Here beside me.

ARKADY There ... beside you?

ANNA Please. [*He does*] You're staring.

ARKADY I was afraid of that.

47

ANNA I just thought I should let you know.

ARKADY Thank you. Excuse me. [*He lowers his head*] You're beautiful.

ANNA So are you.

ARKADY What?

ANNA So have you decided what you're going to do with your life yet?

ARKADY Well I ... How did –

ANNA Bazarov says he's going to hire a band when you make a decision. I would have suggested law from what he told me of your ambitions. Law is the surest route to power unfortunately. But now that I've met you I don't think law is right for you at all. You're far too shy.

ARKADY No ... No ... Not as a rule ... But when I saw you ... I became ... No it's too embarrassing to talk about.

ANNA So we won't.

ARKADY Thank you. So ... you've come to this hotel to be with Bazarov. Actually I'd like to rephrase that if you don't mind.

ANNA You know Bazarov and I have been having an affair for a number of years. We don't have to be coy about that. We can be coy about other things if you wish ...

ARKADY I ... well ... I've often asked to meet you.

ANNA He likes his life compartmentalized. Have you ever met his parents.

ARKADY No.

ANNA Neither have I. He's kept us all separated. At first I believed that he was ashamed of every one of us. But later I understood ...

ARKADY Focus.

ANNA Yes. Exactly. Full attention to each at all times. No compromises for social reasons only.

ARKADY And besides it wasn't necessary.

ANNA [*smiles*] I see we have been reading the same book.

ARKADY Yes he's quite a book our friend. Very demanding.

ANNA And this is precisely the sort of conversation he has prevented us from having.

ARKADY Until now for some reason.

ANNA That was my idea. In fact I insisted upon it. I need help from both of you. [ARKADY *stands*]

ARKADY I am at your service, till death if need be! [*He sits.
Lowers his head*] I'm sorry. What a stupid thing to say.

ANNA Like something out of a romance novel, wasn't it?

ARKADY I used to read those books when I was young. I'm afraid
little pieces of them are still attached to my brain.
[*A commotion outside. Two voices. Then a loud noise*]
[BAZAROV *comes on. Adjusting his clothes*]

BAZAROV [*to* ANNA] Please explain to that moron out there that if a
person has already been in the room it poses no danger
to let him return.

ANNA Did you hurt him badly.

BAZAROV He's ten feet high and weighs as much as a horse. The
best I could do was put a finger in his eye. He'll be fine ...
[*He sits*] So will Viktor. And to prove he's a man of spirit
and balance he sent us another bottle of his father's
best.
[BAZAROV *opens the champagne. Serves*]

ARKADY None for me, please ... It ... makes me foolish.

BAZAROV Really? Since when.

ARKADY Please, no.

BAZAROV Very well. [*to* ANNA] Have you two become intimate
friends yet. Or was he dumbstruck by your appearance.

ARKADY Yes. I behaved like a total ass, you'll be glad to hear.

BAZAROV She has the same effect on all men.

ANNA Not on you, as I remember.

ARKADY But he's not a man. He's a primal force.

BAZAROV I'll take that as a compliment.

ARKADY It was meant as one. Surely you don't believe I enjoy
behaving like a total ass. I'd much rather be a primal
force.

ANNA I thank heaven there is a Bazarov in my life. Although,
heaven knows, one is quite enough.

BAZAROV He won't know how to take that. Arkady is a primal
force in training.

ANNA That's too bad. You make a much more potent team the
way you are. [*to* BAZAROV] That is the way you are. [*to*
ARKADY] And ... the way ... *you* are.

BAZAROV More champagne?

ANNA Yes, please.

ARKADY I'll join you.

BAZAROV Really. Found your footing again, have you? [*He pours*] Go ahead, Anna.

ANNA Yes?

BAZAROV The reason we're all here. You are going to tell us aren't you. Or do we have to guess ... Very well. You want us to murder someone.

[ARKADY *laughs*]

ANNA Yes. Exactly. Good for Bazarov.

[ARKADY *looks at* BAZAROV]

BAZAROV Who is it this time. One of those badgering old lechers who are always chasing you all over Russia.

ANNA He's not a lecher. He's a deeply disturbed man. His name is Pavel Petrovich Kirsanov. And I would like him dead within the week.

ARKADY / BAZAROV But –

BAZAROV But that's his ... No! Consider it done.

ANNA Then let's drink to it.

ARKADY But that's my uncle.

ANNA We know.

BAZAROV Let's drink to it!

[BAZAROV *and* ANNA *raise glasses. Look at* ARKADY. *He looks at them*]

[*Blackout*]

Scene Four

A country road
GREGOR *sitting on the ground. Fiddling with a pistol.*
Hears people approaching. Pulls a kerchief up to cover
his lower face. Hides
BAZAROV *and* ARKADY *come on. Carrying suitcases*

BAZAROV I've told you she doesn't really want us to kill him. We're
to talk to him about her, that's all.

ARKADY That in itself might kill him. He'd be appalled. I'm a bit
appalled just thinking about it.

BAZAROV Your uncle has made a serious mistake. Anna is a
woman of the new age. She has no time for fending off
crazed suitors. She has ambitions. She intends to
become politically influential.

ARKADY A woman?

BAZAROV Would you say that to her face.

ARKADY I mean the odds against that would be astronomical.

BAZAROV Would you say that to her face.

ARKADY I have to sit down. [*He does*] I'm tired. Why do we have
to walk everywhere.

BAZAROV Saves money. Keeps us fit. Get up.

ARKADY No. Besides I'm in no hurry to face my uncle. Honestly, I
just don't think it my place to give him romantic advice.

BAZAROV I'll do it.

ARKADY Oh yes. And gently too I imagine.

BAZAROV I'll state the case. I won't stammer. There'll be no
emotion. A simple understanding will be reached.

ARKADY He'll slap your face or something. That's what his
generation does you know.

BAZAROV Well then I'll slap him back. And I'll keep slapping him
till he listens to reason.

ARKADY Bazarov please. He's my father's brother after all. This
once have pity.

BAZAROV No time for that. Pity excuses weakness.

BAZAROV / ARKADY Confuses the strong.

ARKADY Oh please.

BAZAROV Listen. [*He sits beside him*] The truth is it might be
better if I do it anyway. I know things you don't.

ARKADY Yes I know. Only God knows more than you. And just
barely.

BAZAROV Shut up. I know things about your uncle and Anna. Things she told me in confidence just before we left.

ARKADY Are they ... sordid. I don't want to know.

BAZAROV Anna didn't want you to know either. But I think it's better if you do. Considering how weak you're being. Sometimes a little dose of the truth ...

ARKADY Please just tell me if you're going to tell me.

BAZAROV It appears your uncle, besides being a superfluous human being, is an extremely unhealthy one as well. This great unrequited love of his you mentioned to me ... Well it turns out to have been Anna's mother.

ARKADY Is that possible.

BAZAROV One of life's cruel circular jokes ... He pursued her mother for over a decade through Russia Italy France ...

ARKADY England. Scandinavia. He resigned his commission in the army. He spent his entire inheritance. He –

BAZAROV Yes. But for the moment we're telling this story from Anna's point of view. Her mother was married. Happily says Anna, so we'll give her the benefit of the doubt. And your uncle made her life tragic. Letters. Hired informants. Public scenes. Well you know how that crowd responds to those things. Badly. The husband behaved badly. Anna's mother behaved badly. All their friends behaved badly. It became a bad life all around. Five years ago Anna's mother died. After that nothing was heard of Pavel Petrovich. Until three months ago ... You see he's started it all over again. But now he's directing his obsession towards Anna. And something definitely unhealthy is playing havoc with his brain cells. Anna believes your uncle thinks she is, in fact, her mother ... It has to be stopped. Under any other circumstances I could not care less about something like this. The mad dog ruling class insanely sniffing at each other.

ARKADY I think Anna was right not to tell me. You have no compassion. Can't you imagine how great a love that must have been to have driven my uncle into this state.

BAZAROV Romantic bilge. As I've already told you, Anna has other things on her mind. And she's too important to us to be diverted by this kind of thing.

ARKADY And there it is again. 'Important to us.' Us? What are we?

Are we a populist movement. Are we a political party.
Are we an underground army.

BAZAROV Pick one. Your favourite.

ARKADY I'm serious.

BAZAROV So am I. We could be any of those things. We'll have to
see which one is the most useful.

ARKADY And in the meantime we traipse around the countryside
stomping on people's dreams.

BAZAROV [*smiles*] Small tasks. Easily undertaken. Summer drags
along. We go about our business like good citizens.

ARKADY You go about. I'm staying here.

BAZAROV Get up.

ARKADY No. You don't need me. I'm weak. I'm distracted.

BAZAROV But you've got potential. Anna saw it too.

ARKADY I love her.

BAZAROV What.

ARKADY I love her. I loved her from the moment I saw her.

BAZAROV Please don't say things like that without a knowing
smile. They make me nauseous.

ARKADY I could have been more abstract. I could have couched
it in acceptable words. I could have said I felt a bond or
something like that ... but I ...

BAZAROV Give it up. She's not for you. She's too worldly. Too
cynical. Dead cold at the core. I know ...

ARKADY How do you know. You've told me that your ...
friendship, was only physical.

BAZAROV Only physical? Friendship? What else do you suppose
there is.

ARKADY What are you saying.

BAZAROV She's not for you. She's ... for me.

ARKADY [*He stands*] You love her!?

BAZAROV Yes I guess that would be your word for it.

ARKADY All of a sudden you love someone!? And it has to be
her!? [*He lets himself collapse*]

BAZAROV Are you all right ... Arkady?

ARKADY I don't know how long I can take the stress of being
your friend. [*He puts his head in his hands*]

BAZAROV Get up. Let's go.

ARKADY Yes. Why not.

BAZAROV Arkady?

ARKADY [*standing*] Yes. Head on. I'll follow. Why not. I've got nothing else to do with my life. [*They start off.* GREGOR *jumps out behind them. Pointing his pistol*]

GREGOR Stop! Hands up! Don't turn around.

[ARKADY *obeys.* BAZAROV *turns around*] I said don't turn around.

BAZAROV And who are you to tell me what to do.

GREGOR Can't you see I've got a pistol.

BAZAROV Do I look like I'm blind. [*to* ARKADY] Turn around. And look at the wretched little thing who wants to rob us.

GREGOR Be careful what you say.

BAZAROV Shut up. [*to* ARKADY] Turn around.

ARKADY [*sighs*] Certainly. Whatever you say. [*He turns around*]

BAZAROV Imposing, isn't he. This is where the country is going, I tell you.

GREGOR Give me money.

BAZAROV How much.

GREGOR How much? How much do you have.

BAZAROV Why? Do you just want a portion of it. Not the whole amount?

GREGOR Yes. No. Give me the whole amount.

BAZAROV [*to* ARKADY] You see? They *do* respond if you give them attention. They *can* be educated.

GREGOR And your clothes. I want your clothes too. And your suitcases.

BAZAROV Yes that's the problem, all right. Knowing something leads to wanting something leads to wanting everything. [*to* GREGOR] Slow down my friend. It's a long way to the revolution yet. How about a coin or two to help you get a decent meal.

GREGOR I don't see how you can be so brave when I've got a pistol. Maybe you think I won't use it.

BAZAROV Actually I think you can't use it. I can see from here that it's broken. The screw must have fallen away. The trigger is limp.

[GREGOR *checks. Immediately grabs the barrel of the pistol. Holds it up like a club*]

GREGOR [*backing up*] Stay away from me. I warn you. I'm a cornered rat. I'm a cornered rat.

BAZAROV Such amazing self-esteem. No don't run away. I like you.

GREGOR What did you say.

Michael Riley (Arkady), Robert Bockstael (Bazarov) and John Dolan (Gregor)

BAZAROV Don't you remember me ... I like you ... Actually I love you. [*to* ARKADY] I usually use the word ironically as you know. But this fellow I genuinely love. Remember, friend? The piece of garbage your father's bailiff was beating to a pulp.

GREGOR No that's not me. That's ... someone else. You don't recognize me. I'm wearing a mask.

BAZAROV But you haven't changed your clothes.
[GREGOR *looks down. Pause. Pulls down the mask*]

GREGOR These are the only clothes I've got.

BAZAROV I'm sorry.

GREGOR This is my first robbery. I was going to dress myself in your clothes for my second one. If I'd gotten that far.

ARKADY [*to* BAZAROV] Let's go.

BAZAROV Good idea. [*They start off. To* GREGOR] Come on ... Come on, we're leaving.

GREGOR You want me to come with you.

BAZAROV Of course.

GREGOR To turn me in.

BAZAROV No. No why would I do that. You're one of us. [*to* ARKADY] Isn't he.

ARKADY If you say so.

BAZAROV Come on.

GREGOR [*to* ARKADY] Should I do what he says.

ARKADY Do you have anything better to do.

[GREGOR *runs over.* BAZAROV *puts his arm around him*]

BAZAROV Good man. Here we are then. Together. You'll be all right now. You'll be fed. You'll be clothed. You'll have a nice bed at the house of our friend here. Your future is secure. [*He looks up*] One down. One hundred million to go.

[*They start off*]

GREGOR Why are you doing this.

BAZAROV Because I love you.

[*They leave*]

[*Blackout*]

[*Intermission*]

Scene Five

The Kirsanov garden
PAVEL *and* PIOTR
PAVEL *is more done-up than before. He sits in a wicker
chair smoking a cigarette.* PIOTR *stands beside him.
Holding a tray with two glasses of sherry on it*

PAVEL This will be interesting to us both, Piotr. For different
reasons of course.

PIOTR Yes sir.

PAVEL Imagine we are in a salon in Paris. Surrounded by
intriguing people. Over there the Countess What's-her-
name, on my right the Earl of Gloucester or Leicester or
Alabaster, on my left the Baron and Baroness Von
Somewhere ... You get the picture?

PIOTR Very clearly, sir.

PAVEL You are at my side. You are always at my side ... in the
European fashion. Not so close! [PIOTR *backs up a step*]
Good. Our relationship is formal but cordial. Your
attitude is one of muted insouciance. Mine, of amused
tolerance. I banter with the guests. The topic of
conversation changes quickly and often, without
warning. I follow easily. And you in your own way do
the same. And even if you don't you appear to. You
accomplish this with the eyebrows ... [PAVEL
demonstrates. PIOTR *copies him badly*] I'll teach you
later. In the European fashion I occasionally ask you to
remark. For example, I am asked about my home. I say it
is comfortable but simple and quaint in the style of my
country. Isn't that right, Pierre? You say something
appropriate.

PIOTR Home is where the sheep graze. But the heart ... stays?

PAVEL Too much. But the tone is right. And the tone is just
about everything in Paris. We move on. I make a
comment about servants. You know, the usual
complaint. You could say something witty here, Piotr.
Nothing too witty or you'll appear to have been coached
beyond your class.

PIOTR Sir, with indulgence, wit has nothing to do with class.
It's a gift. I've got it.

PAVEL Suppress it ... Or at least mute it. Mutation is the essence of good conversation.

PIOTR Is mutation the correct word there, sir?

[KIRSANOV *and* BAILIFF *come on arguing*]

KIRSANOV Leave me alone. Stop pestering me.

BAILIFF I need more authority. That's what it comes down to. The serfs are running amok.

KIRSANOV Stop thinking of them as serfs. They're not, you know. They're tenants actually.

BAILIFF They'll always be serfs to me.

KIRSANOV Yes. Yes. Well this is an experimental situation here. And in order for the ... experiment to succeed, certain ... certain ... concessions have to be made. Among them ... well you just have to stop beating them all the time. Beatings. Beatings. Everywhere I go I see the results of your rod or your club. Sometimes it seems half the estate is bleeding to death.

BAILIFF You know the truth is I think they enjoy it as much as I do. It's habit forming, I think.

KIRSANOV What? So you admit you enjoy it.

BAILIFF Sure.

KIRSANOV But ... but don't you think ... Aren't you worried that might make you ... well a bit mentally unstable.

BAILIFF Have you ever beaten anyone.

KIRSANOV No.

BAILIFF You should try it. I bet you'd enjoy it too. It's a good thing. It feels good. I don't know why. I didn't make human beings. Human beings enjoy beating other human beings. That's a fact.

KIRSANOV Well ... well try to stop please. Try to find your pleasure somewhere else ... I'll give you a raise in pay if you cut your beatings in half this month.

BAILIFF They'll rob you blind. They'll get drunk and do damage to the machinery. They'll eat their children ...

KIRSANOV Just try. Think of it as an experiment.

BAILIFF Sure. But you'll see. I'm warning you. Consider yourself warned, all right?

KIRSANOV Yes. Thank you. Goodbye. [BAILIFF *leaves. Sitting*] Could I have one of those glasses.

[PIOTR *hands him one*]

PAVEL Did it ever occur to you, brother, that you weren't cut out for this work.

KIRSANOV Every day ... But I feel something important needs to be done here. I feel I ...

PAVEL Let others do it.

KIRSANOV Men like our bailiff? Men like our corrupt governor? [KIRSANOV *drinks. Groans loudly. Looks at* PIOTR]

PIOTR English sherry, sir.

PAVEL I'll be packing soon. Leaving on a great adventure. You're welcome to come with me.

KIRSANOV Oh don't leave again, Pavel. You know you always return in disrepair.

PAVEL There is a lady who needs my attention, my devotion, my ... protection.

KIRSANOV There's no one ... nothing out there for you anymore.

PAVEL I'm too old for adventure, you think.

KIRSANOV Well no ... Yes. Yes I can't let you go on thinking ... look at you. Why are you wearing all that powder!?

PAVEL It suits me!

KIRSANOV It ... Piotr, go away. [PIOTR *turns around*] No, Piotr. Go. Away! [PIOTR *leaves*] People laugh at you behind your back.

PAVEL What people. There's no one here except us. And Fenichka. Does she laugh at me.

KIRSANOV No. The others.

PAVEL The help? Do I care what the help thinks about me. Really, brother, let's not allow this democratic strain to become ridiculous. Anyway I'm not the problem. You're the problem!

KIRSANOV I'll be fine when I develop a system of management. You're the problem, actually!

PAVEL Very well. Let's agree to leave each other to our own hell. You to sink like compost into the earth! Me to search for a style of life beyond my grasp!

KIRSANOV But ...

PAVEL What?

KIRSANOV Yes but –

PAVEL What!?

KIRSANOV Well the truth is I don't want you to go! I need you here. I need someone. [*Pause*]

PAVEL You have Fenichka.

KIRSANOV I do?

PAVEL You could.

KIRSANOV Yes well ... I tried to talk to her last night. We ... well we're so very different.

PAVEL Do you know something. I've become quite fond of her. I think she's a rare exception to the rule.

KIRSANOV What rule.

PAVEL *The* rule. The one which keeps everyone and everything in its place. I think she'll be good for you.

KIRSANOV Perhaps. But ... I need ... Arkady. I need him to be with me. Especially if you're leaving. I want what I do here to mean more than myself ... Or perhaps I just want to be close to him again for awhile. Before he leaves me forever.

PAVEL Tell him that. He's a generous boy. Always was. Talk to him when he returns.

KIRSANOV They returned late last night. They're still asleep.

PAVEL They? He brought that son of darkness with him.

KIRSANOV Yes. And someone else.

PAVEL Oh wonderful. An invasion. [*He stands*] In that case I'd better go prepare for battle. Excuse me.
[*He leaves*]
[*A rustling*]

KIRSANOV Who's there.
[FENICHKA *steps out from behind a tree. Or a bush or something*]

FENICHKA Only me. I was walking.

KIRSANOV [*standing*] Where's the baby.

FENICHKA Asleep.

KIRSANOV Good. That's good. So you're walking by yourself these days. I'm glad. It's good to get away from him sometimes.

FENICHKA You think so? Why?

KIRSANOV Yes. No ... Well don't you?

FENICHKA I love him very much. I like being with him.

KIRSANOV Of course. I know ... I wasn't suggesting ... I love him too, you know ... If you don't believe me ... I ... Well perhaps I should spend more time with him myself. But I'm so awfully busy.

FENICHKA Nikolai, may I sit down.

KIRSANOV Of course. Didn't I offer you a seat. I'm sure I meant to ...
Please. There. No here. Yes here beside me.
[*She sits*]
[*Pause*]

KIRSANOV So ... this is pleasant. A pleasant morning.

FENICHKA I overheard you talking to your brother about you and ...
me.

KIRSANOV Oh. Well whatever I said about that I didn't mean. Well I
meant it but I didn't explain it. Not properly.

FENICHKA I think I should go away.

KIRSANOV You do?

FENICHKA I don't exactly have a place to go but maybe you could
arrange work for me somewhere.

KIRSANOV No place to go? And you still want to leave. Do you hate
me Fenichka ... for what happened.

FENICHKA You gave me a beautiful baby ... I don't hate you.

KIRSANOV You think I hate you?

FENICHKA I believe you are trapped inside a terrible problem. With
no way out unless I help you ... by leaving.

KIRSANOV But that's not ... I don't want you to go away ... Fenichka
I know I'm an old man. Believe me, I feel it. With all the
problems on the farm – the workers, the bailiff – but
what has that to do with you ... We were talking about ...
Then there's my brother. And my son ... Arkady. Oh I
love him so much.

FENICHKA Excuse me. [*stands*] I hear my baby crying.
[*She leaves*]

KIRSANOV Why is it I never hear the baby crying when she does.
Am I going deaf ... I should have just said something
affectionate to her. Fenichka I love you. I love you
Fenichka. Just like that. She'd stay if I said that simple
thing to her. So it's up to me. All right then I'll do it ...
[*He starts off*] But not now. I have to supervise the
distribution of fertilizer. [*He turns, starts off in the other
direction*] Yes, one of the highlights of my day.
Distributing fertilizer. [*He is gone*]
[FENICHKA *comes back. Sits. Looking off in the direction*
KIRSANOV *went*]
[BAZAROV *comes on. Eating an apple*]

BAZAROV Hello there.

FENICHKA [*She stands*] Excuse me.

BAZAROV [*He grabs her arm*] Not so fast. The baby's not crying. You can't fool me there. I just came from his room. He's sound asleep.

FENICHKA Oh I thought I heard – [*She is trying to remove his hand, with no success*] But if you say you saw him. And that he's fine ...

BAZAROV Will you sit down with me.

FENICHKA If you take away your hand.

BAZAROV If you promise not to run away.

FENICHKA Why would I run away. I'm not afraid of you.
[BAZAROV *smiles. Takes his hand off her arm. Sits*]
[FENICHKA *sits*]
[*Pause*] What were you doing in the baby's room.

BAZAROV Looking. I like babies.

FENICHKA All of them.

BAZAROV Yes. As a matter of fact, I do.

FENICHKA For scientific reasons?

BAZAROV Oh. So you think you know me, do you.

FENICHKA I listened when you were here before ... talking about various things.

BAZAROV And now you're an expert on my motives.

FENICHKA I don't know how to argue with you. I'll just say you struck me as a harsh person.

BAZAROV Really. Didn't I help you when the baby had a chill.

FENICHKA I watched you then. You examined him like a ... a ...

BAZAROV Specimen.

FENICHKA Yes! Not that I wasn't grateful.

BAZAROV Should I have made baby jokes. Laughed. Perhaps even cried. For God's sake. He was sick. I was trying to make him well. Don't be stupid.

FENICHKA I am stupid. I can't help it. [*She stands. He stands. Puts a hand on her shoulder*]

BAZAROV You're not stupid. I'm rude sometimes. An old habit. I apologize.

FENICHKA That's not necessary.

BAZAROV Good. Let's keep talking. [*They sit*] Tell me everything you think about life. Be honest. Take all the time you need.

FENICHKA Why.

BAZAROV You need a reason to talk about what you think?

FENICHKA I need to know why you want to listen.

BAZAROV I could lie. I could make something up about curiosity. But the truth is I'd like an opportunity to just ... look at you. I find you very attractive.

[*Pause*]

FENICHKA Thank you.

BAZAROV Do you find me attractive. [*Pause*] Well.

FENICHKA I am ... not in a position to ...

[*He is reaching for her hand. The sound of people coming. She pushes his hand away*]

[ARKADY *comes on.* GREGOR *is close behind him*]

ARKADY Good morning, Fenichka.

FENICHKA Good morning.

GREGOR Good morning, Fenichka.

FENICHKA Good morning. Do I know you.

ARKADY No. Pretend he isn't here. Bazarov will you tell him to stop following me around.

BAZAROV But I've told him that's exactly what he has to do if he wants to learn how to behave like a gentleman. And that is what he wants.

ARKADY [*to* GREGOR] Is it?

GREGOR [*to* BAZAROV] Is it.

BAZAROV Yes.

GREGOR [*to* ARKADY] Yes.

ARKADY Well then let him follow you around.

BAZAROV I'm no gentleman. [*to* FENICHKA] Am I?

FENICHKA Aren't you.

ARKADY Bazarov, what does that mean.

BAZAROV Ask her.

ARKADY Fenichka?

FENICHKA He's a ... perfect gentleman. I think he's teasing you. [*She stands*]

ARKADY Why are you leaving.

BAZAROV The baby is screaming his lungs out. Can't you hear him.

ARKADY No ...

FENICHKA The baby is asleep. I just want to look in on him. [*to* BAZAROV] If that's all right with you.

[BAZAROV *smiles*]

ARKADY I'll come with you. This would be a good time to have a long look at my little brother, wouldn't it.

FENICHKA You call him your brother?

BAZAROV Yes. And his kindness in doing so is an inspiration to us all.

ARKADY Mind your own business.

BAZAROV Why do people think that what goes on in a family is somehow beyond the criticism of society in general. Is a family above the civil law? No. Then should it be above the natural law, the laws of behaviour?

ARKADY Only when those laws are being imposed by a man who is not only outside the family but outside of society as well.

BAZAROV You're criticizing me a lot these days. Why is that.

ARKADY I'm only trying to be an intelligent disciple. Besides, I still agree with you about all of the big things.

BAZAROV So your patronizing attitude toward this young woman is a little thing.

ARKADY I think you've misread me on that. If you need an example of a patronizing attitude, examine the way you talk to young Gregor here.

BAZAROV [*to* GREGOR] Do I condesc- – Do I talk down to you.

GREGOR What?

BAZAROV Do I talk to you like you're stupid.

GREGOR But I *am* stupid. Why shouldn't you talk to me like that.

BAZAROV [*sighs, puts his head in his hands*] But what about the famous earthy common sense of the peasant. Don't you think you have that.

GREGOR Maybe. But a lot of good it's done me. No sir, you just keep talking to me like I'm stupid and then maybe I'll learn something.

ARKADY He could have a point there.

BAZAROV But it's so deeply buried in the misery of his self-contempt we might never find it.

ARKADY [*to* FENICHKA] Come on. We'll go look at the baby. And we'll have a good talk too.
[*They start off.* GREGOR *starts off too. To* GREGOR] Stay put.
[*They leave*]

[GREGOR *shoves his hands in his pockets*]

BAZAROV Come sit here by me, old friend.

[GREGOR *obeys.* BAZAROV *puts an arm around him*] So how do you like your new life so far. Is it everything you imagined.

GREGOR Breakfast was good. I ate like a pig.

BAZAROV Well these things take time. At lunch try to eat like a monkey. By supper time we'll have you eating like a human being. No I'm sorry I said that.

GREGOR Why?

[PAVEL *comes on. A bit more done-up. He is wearing his most dandified outfit*]

PAVEL Ah here you are.

BAZAROV Yes. And there you are. Incredible as it may seem.

PAVEL Take your time now. Look me over closely. Examine every excess. Savor me. Then attack. I'm ready.

BAZAROV Before you came out I was sitting here wondering what exactly it is about this place that makes me so wretched. Makes me rude to pleasant young women, cruel to my best friends ... and then here you are. The essential truth. The disease in its most virulent form. The extreme edge so to speak.

PAVEL You and I have unfinished business. My style is at stake. I have prepared a lengthy verbal lesson in history for you.

BAZAROV That will have to wait. I have a message for you from Anna Odintsov.

[*Pause*]

[PAVEL *is still*]

PAVEL How do you know this lady.

BAZAROV That's none of your business. I'm more concerned with how you think *you* know her. But we should discuss this in private. I'll send young Gregor here away.

PAVEL Who is he to me. An empty space. Going or staying he remains an empty space. I'll show you how it is done. [*to* GREGOR] You, beggar boy. This man and I are about to have a discussion. You won't hear it. Do you understand?

GREGOR Yes sir.

65

Robert Bockstael (Bazarov) and Richard Monette (Pavel)

PAVEL [*to* BAZAROV] Speak.
[BAZAROV *approaches him. Takes a pack of letters from his pocket*]

BAZAROV These belong to you.
[PAVEL *looks at them*]

PAVEL No. They belong to the dear lady.

BAZAROV They are your letters. She doesn't want them.

PAVEL Then have her return them herself.
[BAZAROV *throws the letters down*]
[PAVEL *stiffens*]

BAZAROV I don't really wish to be cruel to you, you know.

PAVEL Be cruel. That might be easier for both of us.

BAZAROV You are deluded. You believe this woman is her mother.

PAVEL What I believe is beyond your comprehension.

BAZAROV In some stupid abstract way that might be true. But the simple truth is, these letters prove that you think she's her mother. It's possible that you're only playing at this delusion, in a kind of semi-conscious way. You don't strike me as being insane.

PAVEL What would you know about insanity. Only extremely sensitive people reach that exalted state.

BAZAROV That is dangerous romantic garbage. It is dangerous for the lady in question, for the ones who care for you and for yourself. I advise you to stop giving in to this notion. You are not in a exalted state. You are in a feverish state similar to the ones we all experience in adolescence. In short it is simply time to grow up.
[PAVEL *picks up the letters*]

PAVEL If you were a sensitive man I would tell you that I love the lady. I ... loved the lady very much. Her daughter reminds me so much ... What possible harm can I do with such a love.

BAZAROV For one thing you bring unwanted attention on her. I'm talking to you now like you're sane. I'm giving you the benefit of the doubt ... If you listen like a sane person should, it can stop here. If it doesn't stop, I will be forced to take action.

PAVEL A threat. Good.

BAZAROV Believe it or not, except for this matter, I have no real quarrel with you.

PAVEL That's not true. We are enemies!

BAZAROV You are no threat to me, I'm sorry. There is only the matter of your obsessive behaviour toward my friend Anna Odintsov.

PAVEL And other than that, no threat? I don't believe it!

BAZAROV Believe it.

[*Pause*]

PAVEL I see ... Well you have spoken clearly ... I can assure you of one thing at least. The lady has nothing to fear from me. [*He starts off. Stops*] As for the motives behind my 'obsessive behaviour' as you call it –

BAZAROV No explanation please.

PAVEL No, of course not. That would be totally absurd anyway. Almost as absurd as the way I dress.

[*He bows. Leaves*]

BAZAROV Sad.

GREGOR Sad?

[BAZAROV *looks at* GREGOR. *Goes to him. Takes him by the shoulders*]

BAZAROV I'm sorry if I've been cruel to you. I don't mean to be cruel ... Honestly.

[*He pulls* GREGOR *to him.* GREGOR *puts his head on* BAZAROV's *chest*]

[*Blackout*]

Scene Six

Begins in darkness. With a crash
Then the loud sustained sound of eeeeeeeeeeee
Lights
The Kirsanov supper table. KIRSANOV, ARKADY, PAVEL, *and*
FENICHKA *are seated. Watching* SITNIKOV *in a desultory*
manner. SITNIKOV *is standing next to the table*
GREGOR *sits silently beside* BAZAROV *throughout the entire*
scene. Eating slowly. Carefully
BAZAROV *is smiling broadly at* SITNIKOV

SITNIKOV Well of course this could be an extremely embarrassing
moment if we don't look for the humour in it. Eeeeeee. I
mean I barge in here uninvited. I interrupt your supper.
I stumble in my awkwardness and break a decanter –
[PIOTR *rises from behind the table. Holding the broken*
pieces]

PIOTR A decanter. And a two hundred year old bowl.

SITNIKOV Oh a bowl too. I'm so sorry. I apologize. Arkady, who
should I be apologizing to.

ARKADY This is my father.

SITNIKOV I apologize, sir. For the bowl. For the interruption.

BAZAROV Quick Viktor. The humour. Get to the humour of it.

SITNIKOV Well the truth is ... You see I did see the possibility of
humour a moment ago. But it seems to have slipped
away.
[PIOTR *leaves*]

ARKADY I don't suppose you could manage to do the same thing.

SITNIKOV Oh I see. I'm not wanted here. How was I to know.

ARKADY The fact that you weren't invited could have served as a
hint.

SITNIKOV Well you might like to know that I'm on a mission of
honour. [*to* BAZAROV] Not that honour means anything to
me. [*to* KIRSANOV] Not that I have anything against
honour.
[ANNA *comes on. Followed by* SERGEI]

ANNA I asked him to bring me. Arkady, I didn't know where
you lived.

SITNIKOV Madame Odintsov. I was about to explain.
[*The men stand. Except* BAZAROV]

ANNA Yes Viktor. But now I'm putting you out of your misery.

Please gentlemen. Sit. [*Only* GREGOR *sits. Then* GREGOR *rises*] No. Sit!

[*They all sit except* ARKADY]

ARKADY Ah. Father. Uncle. This is –

ANNA Anna Odintsov.

[*She goes to* KIRSANOV. *Puts out her hand. He takes it awkwardly*]

KIRSANOV It is a pleasure to have –

ANNA Yes yes pleasure. I'm sorry to interrupt your supper but I have some urgent business here. [*to* BAZAROV] I realized after all, that it required my personal attention.

BAZAROV That might not be necessary.

[ANNA *akes out a letter. Shows it to* BAZAROV]

ANNA I received that this morning. [*points to* PAVEL] From him.

[BAZAROV *looks at it. At* PAVEL]

KIRSANOV What's going on here.

PAVEL Nothing to do with you Nikolai. [*He stands*] Madame I am at your disposal.

ANNA Somewhere quiet please.

PAVEL The garden should do. [*to others*] Excuse me.

[*They start off*]

ANNA [*over her shoulder*] Oh. And me.

[PAVEL *points the way.* ANNA *goes.* PAVEL *follows her.* SERGEI *follows him*]

KIRSANOV Arkady, do you know what this is about.

ARKADY I think you should ask Uncle Pavel, Father.

BAZAROV That would not be wise. It's quite crowded in the labyrinth already. [*He laughs*]

KIRSANOV So you know about this too? So this is just something else beyond my knowledge. Why am I in the dark about so many things. Am I prematurely senile.

FENICHKA Perhaps it doesn't concern you, Nikolai.

KIRSANOV He's my brother, isn't he. Obviously he's in some kind of dilemma. If I'd had my eyes open I would have seen it ... but ... Fenichka –

FENICHKA What?

KIRSANOV Nothing.

SITNIKOV Excuse me. I seem to have been left dangling here. It's rather awkward.

KIRSANOV [*to* FENICHKA] You. You're the problem.

SITNIKOV Me?

KIRSANOV No not you. Her. Who are you anyway. Never mind. [*to* FENICHKA] My senility. It's because of you Fenichka. You're all I see – what should I do about you.

FENICHKA Please Nikolai. Not now.

BAZAROV Why ask her what you should do anyway.

ARKADY Bazarov.

BAZAROV She's not your conscience. She may be your responsibility but –

KIRSANOV Oh an opinion about that too.

ARKADY Bazarov you have no right to be involved.

BAZAROV But I do.

SITNIKOV Perhaps I could just sit down.

BAZAROV I have a deep and perfect right.

ARKADY And what is it.

KIRSANOV Yes what.

SITNIKOV So no one objects then. [*He sits.* BAZAROV *stands*]

BAZAROV I love her.

KIRSANOV What?

FENICHKA [*to* BAZAROV] Please. Stop.

BAZAROV I love her. And I want to marry her.

ARKADY Bazarov what is this about.

BAZAROV Are you asking me to explain love to you. Very well. It's a kind of deep abiding passion. It makes the earth tremble. It glows in the dark.

FENICHKA Sir. You are going too far. I think you misunderstood my openness.

KIRSANOV What openness? Oh ... I see. Now I finally see something. And it's awful. He's young isn't he. That's the whole truth.

FENICHKA Nikolai, you're being stupid.

BAZAROV Marry me. I'm not stupid.

KIRSANOV I'm dying here. My chest feels like it's twisting inside my skin. I can't breathe.

ARKADY Father.

KIRSANOV No leave me alone ... I'm too old to live.

[KIRSANOV *goes out*]

[ARKADY *starts to follow*]

BAZAROV Stay here. He'll be fine. He's just had a shock.

ARKADY You don't have to tell me what he's just had. You have just ended our friendship.

BAZAROV But I thought you loved me. I thought our bond was

unbreakable. Beyond the reach of history, politics, religion, family.

ARKADY But not cruelty. Or ... disloyalty.

BAZAROV Fenichka tell our friend here that nothing happened between us.

FENICHKA Yes. Nothing, Arkasha. It was a misuse of words on my part.

BAZAROV I *do* love you, though. In a way. You remind me of the sister I never had.

SITNIKOV Eeeeeeeee.

BAZAROV You find that funny, Viktor?!

SITNIKOV [*sobers immediately*] Not if it wasn't a joke.

BAZAROV Fenichka. You know I don't want to marry you.

FENICHKA Why should you.

BAZAROV Well that's another question. I probably should. But I'm hard at the core. Love for just one person isn't strong enough to penetrate.

ARKADY Besides, it's actually only the idea of you he loves. [*to* BAZAROV] Correct?

BAZAROV I suppose so.

ARKADY Grotesque. You become more inhuman every day. Some perverse idea enters your head and you just spew it out and let it bounce off anyone who happens to be there. You toy with the idea of a kind of love for her and you bounce it off my father's skull!

BAZAROV You know I believe that's an accurate observation. I do things like that often. I wonder why. Do you have any ideas?

ARKADY None at all.

BAZAROV Well, in any event you're wrong about me this time. I had an 'honourable' motive. I thought your father just needed a good shock about this young woman here and his true feelings toward her. A little challenge to bring him to his senses.

ARKADY What a brazen reckless thing to do.

BAZAROV I'll bet good money he proposes to her before the night is through.

ARKADY Not if he believes there's something between the two of you.

BAZAROV Don't worry. Fenichka will go tell him the truth about that ... Won't you?

FENICHKA Yes.

[BAZAROV *helps her up*]

BAZAROV She'll gaze lovingly into his eyes and he'll believe every word she says ... Won't he.

FENICHKA Yes.

BAZAROV And she'll do it right now. Very quickly. Before he does something foolish to himself ... Won't you.

FENICHKA Yes! [*She starts off*] And if he believes ... and if that makes him think ... I'll be grateful to you forever.
[*She runs off*]

ARKADY And if it fails I'll cut out your heart.

BAZAROV There's always a risk in meddling in other people's affairs. If you meddle deeply enough. Cut right into the heartland of hypocrisy.

ARKADY That's what you think you've done to my father, is it.

BAZAROV If it turns out well, does it matter. Listen. That thing between them was not going in the direction of resolution.
[ARKADY *sits*]

ARKADY I'd feel better if I thought you did these things out of concern and not just to exercise your brain.

BAZAROV Drink? Come on, drink. A few vodkas will take the hard edge off the argument I know we are about to have.

ARKADY I've decided never to drink with you again.
[BAZAROV *fills two glasses with vodka*]
[*Lights fade in the drawing room*]
[*Lights up in the garden*]
[PAVEL *is sitting.* ANNA *is pacing slowly*]

ANNA ... and so when I received your letter this morning my heart sank. I was sure that when Bazarov had explained to you how I felt I would hear nothing more from you. This has to stop. You have terrorized and destroyed my family. And I won't let you terrorize and destroy me.

PAVEL Please. I have to interrupt. I am extremely uncomfortable with this situation.

ANNA You are responsible for this situation.

PAVEL I meant our physical situation. I am sitting while you stand. Perhaps if you sat or if you allowed me to join –

ANNA Never mind that. You are fine where you are. I am fine where I am.

PAVEL Well at least I can see the moonlight in your hair.

ANNA Please.

PAVEL Your sparkling eyes, the fluidity of your movements.

ANNA Please!

PAVEL I only wish to add that you dress well. You dress with simplicity and style.

ANNA Have you no sense at all!? Are you totally incapable of having a reasonable conversation!? Of receiving information!?

PAVEL I ... didn't mean to be disrespectful.

ANNA That's not the point. [*pause*] Listen to me. Perhaps you think my objections to the ... attention you're giving me aren't serious enough. That they are only signs of girlish coyness.

PAVEL You are not a girl. I know that.

ANNA But do you know that the difficulties you are causing me are not ones that I can just casually dismiss. What I am doing with my life now is full of risk ... I wish I could trust you enough to tell you the truth about myself ... If you knew the truth you'd hate me. No! What I really want to say to you, what you should be able to understand, is that I'm afraid. To be the object of your desire against my will, is in some way I can't quite explain, terrifying. Do you want to terrify me, Pavel Petrovich.

PAVEL No of course not.

ANNA Then stop this immediately.

PAVEL If I could ... but –

ANNA Are you admitting that you are too weak to stop.

PAVEL Weak? I feel a great strength in my feelings toward you.

ANNA Perhaps you need an even greater strength to *control* your feelings.

PAVEL Perhaps. But did you read my last letter?

ANNA Of course.

PAVEL Carefully?

ANNA Carefully? No. I was only looking for an apology.

PAVEL Ah. But I wasn't offering an apology. I was offering an explanation. May I have it.

ANNA [*sighs*] If you wish.

[*She hands it to him. He unfolds it*]

PAVEL Yes here it is. Perhaps this might explain for you.
[*reading*] 'And yet there's something about me you
cannot know. The love I felt for your mother was my life.
It came to be my entire life. No thoughts in my head. No
world in front of my eyes. No friends. Or family. Or
profession. I only lived in my love for your mother.
Which drew me to her, so close that everything in the
world came through her and I was just an aura, not
solid, not heard ... and finally not felt. And when she was
gone from me ... I began to dissolve ...' [*He looks at her*]
And then I saw you and I stopped dissolving and after I
stopped dissolving I began to hope that I could become
real again. To let the force of love make me ... real ...
[*He drops the letter*]
[*He puts his hand over his eyes*]
I'm sorry.

ANNA If you have the strength to love that way, you have the
strength to attract a love in return someday that is also
... real.

PAVEL Unfortunately that's not how it works ... I'm too old ...
too ... unhealthy in my mind. Too weak, yes I know that.
And ... I'm dissolving again.
[*He sits. Lowers his head*]
[ANNA *sits*]
[*Pause*]

ANNA You could read me more of the letter. If you want to. I
mean that might help you.

PAVEL How?

ANNA To understand your state of mind. Or it might help me
to understand ... or maybe we could find someone
who'd understand. And then we could talk again.
[*She picks up the letter. Sits again. Hands it to him*]
Go ahead.
[*Lights fade*]
[*Lights up in the drawing room*]
[BAZAROV *and* ARKADY *seem more relaxed. A bit drunk. So
are* GREGOR *and* SITNIKOV]

BAZAROV Go ahead. Say it.

ARKADY No you go ahead.

BAZAROV Just say it. Go on –

[SITNIKOV *jumps to his feet*]

SITNIKOV   I have to say that even though I'm ignorant of many of the specific details, that is, when one of you says 'he' and the other one 'she' I don't know who you are talking about, nevertheless I've found the conversation so far, very stimulating. I have to agree with Bazarov of course.

BAZAROV / ARKADY   Of course.

SITNIKOV   Eeeeeeee. No seriously. I mean ... take hypocrisy as an example. It's everywhere isn't it. It's one of the things we'll always have to be on guard against. Treat it like an enemy. Show no mercy. Never bend. Difficult, to say the least. But we'll manage as long as we stick together. We'll be a force of truth and courage. And honesty.

BAZAROV   Where did you get that fancy new coat.

SITNIKOV   I stole it from my father. Eeeeeee. No I made that up. You see I can make a joke as well as anyone. You have to stop underestimating me. No the coat was a gift from Madame Odintsov. It belonged to her late husband.

BAZAROV   The one who died of leprosy?

[SITNIKOV *stiffens*] Eeeeeeeee.

SITNIKOV   I knew you were joking that time. I warn you. I'm getting harder to trick every day.

[BAZAROV *smiles*]

ARKADY   Why would the lady give you a coat, Viktor.

SITNIKOV   I asked for it ... Well people were always making fun of my other coat. I found it difficult to get them to take me seriously.

BAZAROV   Coward. You always told us you were a Slavic nationalist. And it was your duty to dress like a Slav.

SITNIKOV   But the truth is I'm not a Slav. And now I have the courage to admit it.

ARKADY   So why were you pretending to be one in the first place.

SITNIKOV   Because they were the only ones who invited me to join their political party. Yes. And now I have the courage to admit that too ... I think I'm making great strides don't you.

BAZAROV   [*stands*] But in what direction, Viktor!?

[ANNA *comes on. She looks shaken*]

ANNA   Pour me something to drink please.

[ARKADY *obliges.* ANNA *sits*] I feel as if I've just done something very cruel. And I'm not sure why.

BAZAROV I take it he didn't respond well.

ANNA He wouldn't –

ARKADY Excuse me. Viktor this is personal business we are going to discuss.

SITNIKOV Of course. I'll be discreet.

ARKADY You'll leave the room.

SITNIKOV Of course. [*He stands*] Where am I going. Am I staying the night. Am I going somewhere else for the night.

ARKADY You're just leaving the room.

SITNIKOV Of course.

[*He leaves*]

ANNA What about him. [*points to* GREGOR]

BAZAROV He stays at my side. Forever. He is my future. Continue.

ANNA He wouldn't listen to me at first. But at some point I thought we'd reached an agreement of sorts. Then ... the letter. He read it to me ... It was ... It was all of his heart I think. And his soul and his life. It just poured out. Page after page of excruciating personal disclosure and pleading for my love. In language I have never heard before. So tightly strung ... emotional ... almost raving ... building to some kind of terrifying climax. I could feel it coming like a wind. Like energy. I felt as if it was going to leap off the page and kill one of us ... both of us ... but suddenly he ... just stopped ... Then he ran off.

[*Pause*]

[ARKADY *stands*]

ARKADY I should go find him.

ANNA I told Sergei to follow him. And to make sure he did no harm to himself.

[ARKADY *sits*]

BAZAROV Your uncle might be insane.

ARKADY You'd say that, I know.

BAZAROV [*to* ANNA] What would you say.

ANNA He scares me. I know that. But I don't think he's insane. He has a pure obsession and he's let it take him away.

ARKADY It's only love. A little thing. Not a nightmare. Not a huge screaming storm. It's a little precious feeling. I understand him I think.

BAZAROV Not now, Arkady. Save that talk for when there's less at stake. Anna's safety for example.

77

ARKADY   When is there ever anything not at stake. When can you have a feeling and not put something at risk. If you keep denying the true passion in people, Bazarov, you'll never be the great leader all your friends expect. If you can't forgive my uncle, how will you be able to forgive the hundred million.

BAZAROV   But it's not a matter of forgiving your uncle. I'm trying to protect Anna.

ARKADY   I don't entirely believe that. What's burning in my uncle will dissolve eventually and I think you know that. You see again, it's what you call the general idea behind his feelings you want to destroy. An idea which you find very threatening because it's beyond your own comprehension.

BAZAROV   [*He stands*] This is getting us nowhere. We still have a problem. If you have a problem. Solve it. I thought I taught you that much.

ARKADY   Oh. Very well. Anna. This will be totally unexpected. Perhaps shocking. Perhaps absurd. Will you marry me.

ANNA   I beg your pardon.

BAZAROV   Come on, Arkady. Doesn't she have enough of that to deal with already.

ARKADY   [*to* ANNA] I don't think you are your mother. I know exactly who you are. And who I am. And what I feel.

BAZAROV   Stop this, now.

ARKADY   Shush! I feel something special for you, Anna. I felt it immediately. Yes. Like they do in those silly romantic novels. I think I could make you happy. I'm different from Bazarov in important ways. I know that now. I could be a healthy strong anchor for you. I respect everything you are trying to do and will offer any assistance I can. As well as a life-long devotion to your happiness and well-being. So I am asking you to marry me even if you don't love me because much good will come to both of us if you do.

BAZAROV   Wonderful. And what do you possibly expect her to say to something like that.

ANNA   I'll think it over. [*They both look at her*] I mean he makes perfect sense when you listen to him closely.

BAZAROV   Are you serious.

ANNA   Serious enough to give it some consideration. I know
Bazarov that you and I could never be happy. And you
know that too.

BAZAROV   I do?

ANNA   We have too much in common. A history together which
was both too frivolous and intense. Besides marriage
might be a good thing for me. My current status in
society seems to be making me vulnerable in many
ways. [*to* ARKADY] I'm much older than you.
[BAZAROV *has moved away a few feet. He is staring off*]

ARKADY   A few years. It means nothing.

ANNA   Oh it could mean something. We would just have to
turn it to our advantage.

BAZAROV   [*to* GREGOR] I feel a certain kind of justice taking place
here.

ARKADY   I'm in shock. I never imagined you'd say yes.

ANNA   I haven't said yes.

ARKADY   I know. But now I can imagine that you will.

BAZAROV   I could have imagined it easily, if I'd taken the time.
Another one of life's cruel circular jokes.

ARKADY   Do you think you'll be taking a long time to make up
your mind.

ANNA   Oh no. A few days at the most. Now I warn you not to
get your hopes up. I'm not a fickle person but I could be
swayed by practicalities beyond your control.

ARKADY   If it's all right with you, I think I'll get my hopes up
anyway. It will be a new sensation for me.

BAZAROV   Well I can learn to live with it. In fact, I'm starting to
enjoy the idea already a bit. [*He looks at them*] Of course
you'll have children. And name one after me.

ARKADY   Of course.

ANNA   If you wish.

BAZAROV   That was a joke actually.

ANNA   Oh.

ARKADY   Oh.
[FENICHKA *comes on*]

FENICHKA   He's disappeared. Nikolai. I couldn't find him anywhere.
He's wandering around thinking I've been unfaithful to
him. What do you think he'll do. No don't tell me.
[SERGEI *comes on*]

Diane D'Aquila (Anna) and Robert Bockstael (Bazarov)

SERGEI That man you had me following ma'am. Well I didn't do so good a job. Gone like a puff of smoke. [*to* GREGOR] I think the wood demons got him.
[GREGOR *stands, knocking over his chair*]
[BAZAROV *stares off*]

BAZAROV Pile them on. One after the other. If fate's a comedian we've got one hell of a big laugh in store. If he's feeling tragic well ... what can I say.

ARKADY I don't understand what you're talking about. Or why you're talking about it at this particular moment. [*to others*] Come on. We'll organize a search party.
[GREGOR *and* SERGEI *don't move*] Come on!

SERGEI No. I ain't goin' up against the wood demons.
[ARKADY *groans. Grabs them. And they all rush off. Except* ANNA *and* BAZAROV]
[BAZAROV *goes to the table. Stands behind* ANNA. *She hands him her drink*]

ANNA [*laughs*] Chaos in the country. This is just the sort of thing we should enjoy.

BAZAROV I'd prefer their world to crumble without causing pain. I find no pleasure in human misery.

ANNA Perhaps that's because you haven't met the true enemy yet. He's waiting for us in the cities.

BAZAROV Are you seriously considering Arkady's proposal.

ANNA Which one of us are you worried about.

BAZAROV You see the thing we both find attractive about him, the thing that makes him different from you and me, is his ability to let his heart make little compromises with the truth ... Will you tell him that you are planning to use bombs, Anna ... that you've already used one or two.

ANNA Of course.

BAZAROV What do you suppose he'll do then.

ANNA Choose.

BAZAROV [*laughs*] Now that will be hard won't it. Because I believe he really loves you. Yes, that will be a hard choice. Or a hard compromise. [*shakes his head*] Excuse me. I've never seen a search party organized before. [*He starts off*] And I've always wondered how it was done. Oh, by the way. [*He stops*] I love you too.
[*Pause*]

ANNA Am I supposed to say something now.

BAZAROV Well it occurred to me ... that ... you might not have known that.

ANNA [*She stands*] So you actually believe I am considering marriage to Arkady because I think you don't love me. I explained to you why I might marry him. I thought my reasons were both personally and politically clear. If the same sort of thing had come from your mouth there would have been no further questions ... You have to start listening to me. And you have to start believing what I say!

[*Pause*]

BAZAROV Yes. You're right. I'm sorry.

ANNA [*smiles*] So do you still love me.

BAZAROV More than ever.

ANNA If it's important to you, we could talk about it sometime.

BAZAROV Anna. I said I loved you. I never said it was important.

[*He leaves*]

[*Blackout*]

Scene Seven

Midnight
In the woods
The light of a full moon
PIOTR, GREGOR, SERGEI, *and the* BAILIFF *come on. Carrying*
torches

PIOTR Watch where you're walking, fool. You'll set someone on fire.

SERGEI Is he talking to me.

GREGOR No I think he's talking to me.

PIOTR Shush ... Stop!

SERGEI He *is* talking to me.

GREGOR No he's —

PIOTR Listen! [*They do*] Who hears what I hear.

GREGOR What do you hear.

SERGEI Is it the sound of someone being eaten alive?

PIOTR Silence.

GREGOR He hears silence.

SERGEI The wood demons and the shadow monsters all eat people whole. Is it a crunching sound.

PIOTR Nothing. All right. Everyone spread out.

BAILIFF I say if they wanted to get lost we should leave them lost. Who cares about those two snotty old guys, anyway.

PIOTR I do. You should too. They pay your wages.

BAILIFF I've got talent. I can get a job anywhere.

SERGEI The moon is full. But it's yellow. That's a kinda unnatural colour for a moon isn't it.

GREGOR Is it.

BAILIFF Maybe. Maybe not. I'm not saying.

PIOTR I said spread out. Why isn't anyone spreading out.

GREGOR I think you have to tell us more than that. Suppose we all spread out the same way.

PIOTR God help us all.

SERGEI Yeah, let's pray. I know one that keeps the spirits of the undead from sneaking into you through your mouth. They go in that way cause a man's mouth is always wide open when he meets the undead.

PIOTR Spread out! You that way. You that way. You this way. [*They begin to move off. Slowly fanning out*]

GREGOR If I find them what do I say. I can't just tell them to go home. Who am I to tell them where to go or not to go.

PIOTR Just say that supper is ready. They'll get the hint.

GREGOR What hint. If that's a hint I don't get it myself.

PIOTR It's a discreet way of saying people are worried about them.

BAILIFF I'm not worried about them. They're nothing to me. Like I'm nothing to them. We're two halves of a thing that doesn't exist ... And I still don't see why we have to be doing this anyway.

PIOTR I volunteered us.

BAILIFF Typical. One go-getter always volunteers. And he always takes a few lackeys with him, against their will. That's how go-getters get things. And that's how lackeys get to stay lackeys.

PIOTR [*backing off*] Spread out! And keep spreading out until you disappear from the face of the earth!!
[*They are all offstage now. Except* SERGEI *who has paused briefly*]

SERGEI I see a terrible darkness. I feel a frightful stillness. Oh oh, now I hear it ... I hear ... the silence. [*He starts off slowly*] Demons be kind. I'm big ... but I'm confused.
[*And* SERGEI *is off now too*]
[*Silence*]
[*A lamp is lit behind a tree.* PAVEL *steps out. Holding the lamp and a flask of vodka. He is a bit drunk*]

PAVEL My life just stumbled across my eyes. All Russia is searching for her wayward son. I am moved by her concern. Worried a bit about her competence. [*He sits against a tree*] I was right behind this tree you pitiful collection of half-eaten non-entities!! Ah ... but I love you still a bit. Do you still love me a bit. Does anyone love me. Ah that's too sad a question ... If you think that's sad imagine the answer ... Oh no keep the mouth closed or the undead will be climbing in by the droves. [*He falls over laughing*] If she could see me now. [*He sits up*] Maybe she should see me now. A little pity goes a long way for a woman. But not her. God, she is hard. Is she some new invention. Yes she is a hard new thing. Ah forget her. Who can I love instead.

[KIRSANOV *comes on. Wrapped in a horse blanket*]

KIRSANOV Pavel?

PAVEL I know this man. I knew him in better times.

KIRSANOV Pavel. Is that you.

PAVEL Forget you saw me. Spread a rumour that I'm dead. Go get your supper. Tell them to call in the search party.

KIRSANOV The search party is for me.

PAVEL Me as well! Why are you wearing a horse blanket.

KIRSANOV Cold.

PAVEL And sad?

KIRSANOV Can I join you.

PAVEL You are my brother. I love you. Yes! You are one of the things I love. Come here. Sit down. [KIRSANOV *obeys*] Let me hug you.

KIRSANOV Are you drunk, Pavel.

[PAVEL *passes him the flask.* KIRSANOV *drinks*]

PAVEL What is Russia. No what is the world. Is the world just ... future. Is the future a hard place to be.

KIRSANOV Probably. Yes.

PAVEL Not for you. You have love.

KIRSANOV So you haven't heard what's happened.

PAVEL News doesn't travel very fast in the forest. I've tried to keep up but – No, I'm sorry. I'm drunk. Tell me.

KIRSANOV Fenichka loves Bazarov.

PAVEL Don't be stupid. She loves you.

KIRSANOV She feels obligated to me. She loves Bazarov.

PAVEL He's a disease. No one loves a disease. Trust me. I'm an expert on love. Actually that's not true is it. I'm more an expert on the absence of love. Go away, I can't help you. You're just making me sadder than I already was.

KIRSANOV I'm sorry.

PAVEL No. Stay put. What are brothers for. Tell me all the sordid details. He molested her, didn't he.

KIRSANOV No I don't think so.

PAVEL Nothing you say will convince me that he didn't, in some cunning nihilistic way, molest her.

KIRSANOV I think they merely found one another. Shared something. I have a vague picture in my mind of how it happened. I've been wandering around for hours picturing it ... vaguely.

David Fox (Kirsanov) and Richard Monette (Pavel)

PAVEL   If it's true, it's too sad to even think about. I don't want you to think about it ... Oh damn the way things are ... if this is how they are ... damn them to hell.

KIRSANOV   Yes. Damn the women and children. Damn the serfs. Damn the farm.

PAVEL   I know. Let's kill each other. One final noble act. I'll make all the arrangements.

KIRSANOV   I appreciate the gesture. But ... I'm not sure I want to die.

PAVEL   Of course you do. What have you got to live for.

KIRSANOV   Well ... there's my son.

PAVEL   He's part of the army of darkness. Do you think he'll have time for you when he's busy setting fire to all the beautiful buildings in Moscow. And Petersburg. Ah that architecture. How can they even consider destroying things of such monumental grace and strength.

KIRSANOV   The thing is ... I think all this is my own fault. Fenichka and I could have been married months ago if I weren't so foolish.

PAVEL   Marriage is just another institution to our friend Bazarov. He would have knocked it down if it was in his way ... Remember the way father conducted his business ...

KIRSANOV   Business? Father was a general in the army, Pavel.

PAVEL   The business of his life. He conducted it with dignity. He behaved well because he knew what he came from. And he knew what he came from was respected. And so it followed that he showed respect ... but I've made this argument before. Who listens.

KIRSANOV   I do.

PAVEL   Remember the holidays. Each holiday marked by the same traditional routine. It gave you strength. It gave you memory ... Oh I ruined that part of my life myself. Ruined any chance to have a real family. I got carried away by love. I couldn't help myself.

KIRSANOV   You could have if you'd wanted to.

PAVEL   Yes. You're right. I enjoyed very much the feeling of being carried away. But only at the beginning. Does everything turn dark in this world, Nikolai.

KIRSANOV   Yes. Darkness. Then ... what?

PAVEL   Death ... Can I hug you again, Nikolai.

KIRSANOV   Yes.

[PAVEL *puts his arm around* KIRSANOV. *Puts* KIRSANOV's *head on his chest*] All I have to stay alive for is my farm.

PAVEL   [*laughs, sighs*] Your pathetic farm.

KIRSANOV   I know now that I wanted a wife and child to live for. Too late though.

PAVEL   Too late. For you. And for me.

KIRSANOV   There's a world of difference between living for something and just staying alive for something.

PAVEL   I'd settle for a reason for staying alive.

KIRSANOV   Promise me you won't kill yourself, Pavel. I couldn't stand it. That would be the last straw for me.

PAVEL   Maybe that's reason enough. At least for now. For tonight. Under this tree ... Are you crying, Nikolai ... There. There. [*He is rocking slowly back and forth*] Please don't. Please ... Nikolai ... Shush ... there, there ... I think the world should be kinder to fools.
[*Blackout*]

Scene Eight

Dawn
An open field
BAZAROV and GREGOR are sitting. Talking. Chuckling. Eating
apples
PAVEL and PIOTR come on
PAVEL in shirt, trousers, and boots
PIOTR is carrying a case
BAZAROV and GREGOR stand

PAVEL Ah you're here. I'm so glad.
[*PAVEL goes to* BAZAROV. *Extends a hand.* BAZAROV
hesitates. Then takes it. They shake] I was worried that
you might not see the note.

BAZAROV You could have knocked. You didn't have to leave an
envelope under my door.

PAVEL It was late. You were asleep. I am, believe it or not, a
considerate man.

BAZAROV Yes. Well here I am. You wanted to talk?

PAVEL This is a bit irregular, I realize. These things are usually
discussed well in advance. What are your feelings about
the old way of settling accounts.

BAZAROV Excuse me?

PAVEL Duelling.

BAZAROV Ah. I see. [*He looks around*] Yes. Dawn. An open field.
Your second.

PAVEL Usually one uses a gentleman as a second. But under
the circumstances, Piotr will have to do.
[PIOTR *bows deeply*]

BAZAROV And the circumstances are?

PAVEL A need for a quick resolution.

BAZAROV To what?

PAVEL In a moment. First. Are you opposed to duelling.

BAZAROV I don't see how that matters much. If there are things
which must be settled they'll be settled somehow.

PAVEL Glad to hear that. Saves me the indignity of having to
whack you about a bit to force your hand.

BAZAROV You want to kill me for some reason, I take it.

PAVEL Please. Killing you isn't the object here. This is a matter
of honour.

BAZAROV Yours?

PAVEL This is not about me. You have dishonoured my brother. How shall I put this delicately.

BAZAROV Why bother.

PAVEL Please. Let me keep some things in my world intact. This is about you and ... the girl. Fenichka.

BAZAROV But there's nothing ...

PAVEL Yes?

BAZAROV Not really. This is not really about that at all for you. Be honest now. If you're honest with me, I might oblige.

PAVEL But this *is* for my brother. And yes! For myself as well. I have to show you somehow that my belief in certain traditions is not just decoration.

BAZAROV Why.

PAVEL Because I *am* a threat to you. I must be a threat to you. I owe it to Russia.

BAZAROV No. You owe it to your father. You owe it to your family, your class, your history. I have absolutely no respect for any of those things. But I have boundless respect for the inevitable. And for Russia. Let's do it!
[BAZAROV *moves toward* PIOTR] Now I take it Piotr has the weapons in this case.

PAVEL Can you shoot well.

BAZAROV I can do everything well.

PAVEL I am a crack shot.

BAZAROV Yes you've told me that before. But you told me so many preposterous things, it's difficult for me to get impressed.

PAVEL Choose your weapon.

BAZAROV There are four pistols here. Are we expecting company.

PAVEL Piotr will explain. Just choose one.
[BAZAROV *does*]

BAZAROV Gregor. Go stand opposite Piotr.

GREGOR Why.

BAZAROV [*to* PAVEL] Can you tell him.

PAVEL The form of it. That's all. The form of it.

BAZAROV Yes the form of it, Gregor. Now get over there.
[GREGOR *obeys*] Now isn't there something about paces involved here.

PAVEL   It is Piotr's duty to explain the rest.

PIOTR   My pleasure. I have made a mark on the ground. There.
That is the centre. The two gentlemen can then mark off
eight or ten paces from that mark. There must be an
agreement here.

PAVEL   Eight?

BAZAROV   Eight is fine.

PAVEL   [*to* PIOTR] Go on.

PIOTR   [*to* BAZAROV] The two gentlemen then raise their
weapons. And shoot when they wish. That should be
the end of you ... it.

PAVEL   You forgot the reason for the other two pistols.

PIOTR   Sorry, sir. If that is not the end of it the two gentlemen
have the option to take another pistol and fire again.

BAZAROV   In the meantime, Piotr, are you reloading the original
pistols. Is this meant to go on all day? There was an
interesting natural science textbook I was hoping to
finish this afternoon.

PAVEL   There will be a maximum of four shots.

BAZAROV   Well I suppose someone should be dead by then.

PAVEL   [*taking his position*] Please honour me by taking this a
little more seriously.

BAZAROV   [*taking his position*] Please honour me by allowing me to
take it any damn way I choose.
[*They are back to back. They move to* PIOTR's *command*]

PIOTR   One ... Two ... Three ... Four –

GREGOR   I can't watch this.

BAZAROV   Is it necessary that he watch.

PAVEL   Under proper circumstances yes. But I think we can
make an exception here.

BAZAROV   Close your eyes, Gregor.

GREGOR   Thank you, sir. [*He does*]

PIOTR   Five ... Six ... Seven ... Eight ...

PAVEL   [*stopping*] Are you there yet.

BAZAROV   Yes. What about one more. Would you mind just one
more.

PAVEL   Fine.

PIOTR   Nine.
[*They both turn*]

[PAVEL *shoots instantly*]

BAZAROV Missed. You were aiming for my head. I felt the bullet whiz by my ear.

PAVEL Shoot.

BAZAROV Not satisfied yet?

PAVEL You must shoot ... and you must do it seriously.

BAZAROV Seriously.

[BAZAROV *looks away. Shoots without aiming.* PAVEL *grabs his leg and falls to the ground*] Oh damn. [*He runs to* PAVEL] Here let me help you up.

PAVEL I can manage. [*He struggles to his feet*]

BAZAROV Well, honour is served then. Now let's get you home and I'll bandage that leg and arrange for a doctor.

[PAVEL *is limping towards* PIOTR]

BAZAROV Where are you going.

[PAVEL *takes another pistol*] Oh I see. Honour really does need to kill someone.

PAVEL Arm yourself.

[BAZAROV *shrugs. Goes and gets a pistol.* PAVEL *has taken his centre position mark again*]

BAZAROV Can't we dispense with the pacing this time.

PAVEL No! We'll do it right!

[BAZAROV *takes his position*]

PIOTR [*more quickly*] One ... two ... three ... four ...

BAZAROV This joke is out of control.

PIOTR Five ... six ...

BAZAROV I think something nasty is going to happen here now.

PIOTR Seven ... eight.

PAVEL We have to do it right. I have to do something right don't you see.

[PAVEL *turns*]

BAZAROV God you're pathetic! [*and he turns, gesturing*] Can't you see I've just been trying –

[PAVEL *shoots*]

[BAZAROV *is thrown back a step. Clutches his chest. Looks down*] Oh wonderful.

[BAZAROV *falls*]

[GREGOR *rushes to him*]

[PAVEL *rushes to him, holding his leg*]

BAZAROV You ... interrupted what I was trying to say.

PAVEL I thought you were going to shoot. I didn't mean to do this. I was going to fire wide. You startled me.

BAZAROV I'm sorry.

PAVEL This looks like a serious wound.

BAZAROV Serious? [*chuckles*] Well I'm glad I was finally able to ... enter into the spirit of the thing. I'm losing ... consciousness now ...
[*He passes out*]

PAVEL Quickly. The two of you. Get him back to the house.
[GREGOR *and* PIOTR *are picking* BAZAROV *up*] Careful. Careful.

PIOTR Good shot, sir.

PAVEL Shut up.

GREGOR Is he dying.

PIOTR Serves him right.

GREGOR Shut up.

PAVEL Quickly. Quickly.
[*They leave*]
[PAVEL *stares after them a moment*]
I didn't mean to do that.
[*He limps off*]
[*Blackout*]

Scene Nine

A bedroom
A bed, a chair, a small table with a lamp on it
BAZAROV *is propped up in bed. His chest bandaged. Blood*
seeping through
ANNA *sits on the edge of the bed. Applying cold*
compresses to his forehead
ARKADY *is in the chair. His head in his hands*

ANNA I can't get the fever down this way. I think that doctor was a quack. I think we should send to town for silver nitrate.

ARKADY Yes. I'll go myself.
[BAZAROV *opens his eyes. He speaks slowly, softly*]

BAZAROV Stupid. All wrong. Silver nitrate is for infections in the blood. My diagnosis is ... a collapsed lung. Ruptured artery ...

ANNA Don't talk.

BAZAROV Then stop playing doctor. Let me die in peace. Silver nitrate. [*He laughs*] Ahh. That hurts.

ARKADY We're worried that the doctor was incompetent.

BAZAROV He was trained by barbarians. Our medical profession is still in the dark ages. I was hoping to help change –

ARKADY You will ...

BAZAROV Please. Try this once only to say useful non-sentimental things. I'm worried about your father.

ARKADY Fenichka found him and they had a long talk. You were right. He's changed somehow.

BAZAROV Oh ... I doubt that. He's going to marry her though.

ARKADY Yes. Probably.

BAZAROV Well that's change enough. Fathers. Did I ever tell you about my father.

ARKADY Never.

BAZAROV Did I ever tell you about him, Anna?

ANNA No.

BAZAROV Well I don't see why I should start now ... No that was a joke ... My father loves me. He's a good man. Retired army doctor ... good doctor ... limited knowledge ... and my mother, she's there still. Good woman. Good cook.

But all I really know about them is ... they love me.
[*He passes out*]

ARKADY Is he dead. God. Is he dead.

ANNA Unconscious ... This is a waste. He's going to die and it's such a waste.
[FENICHKA *and* KIRSANOV *come on*]

KIRSANOV How is he doing.
[*No response*] I'm sorry for you, son.
[BAZAROV *opens his eyes*]

BAZAROV It's getting crowded in here ... Oh look two pairs of soon to be newlyweds ... a matched set ...

KIRSANOV He's delirious. He's seeing double.

ARKADY No. He means Anna and me. I'll explain later.
[ARKADY *goes off*]

BAZAROV I wish I could be there to hear it. Nikolai Petrovich. Can you hear me.

KIRSANOV Yes.

BAZAROV My brain is a step behind my mouth. I'm afraid I'm not coherent.

KIRSANOV You're speaking well.

BAZAROV Good. Anna here is a fine woman. Ignore everything you hear about her reputation. In fact ignore what I just said. I'm delirious.
[ARKADY *comes back on*]

ARKADY Bazarov. My uncle is outside. He wants something from you.

BAZAROV I think I've given your uncle enough for one lifetime. No, I'm wrong. Let him in.
[ARKADY *goes out*] Hello, Fenichka.

FENICHKA I'm sorry. [*to* KIRSANOV] I don't know what to say to him.
[*to* BAZAROV] Can I get you anything.

BAZAROV Yes. Another death. Any other death but this will do. You look wonderful Fenichka. Oh I hear the baby crying.

FENICHKA You do?

KIRSANOV Never mind. He's delirious.

BAZAROV No one ever gets my best jokes ... Oh that reminds me. Where's Viktor.

ANNA Out in the hall. He's afraid to come in. He's worried he'll make a fool of himself.

BAZAROV But that's exactly what he's supposed to do. Please someone ... get him.

FENICHKA I'll go.

[FENICHKA *goes out*]

[ARKADY *and* PAVEL *come in*]

BAZAROV People coming in. Going out. Better actually. Less like a death bed. More like a train station.

KIRSANOV [*laughs loudly*] Very funny, Bazarov.

BAZAROV Thank you.

[KIRSANOV *bows*]

ARKADY My uncle is here, Yevgeny.

PAVEL [*to* BAZAROV] Sir. Young gentleman ... I'm ... leaving here soon. Off on another great journey. My bags are packed ... but ... I find I'm missing something. [*He sits on the edge of the bed. Head bowed*] I need your forgiveness, I'm afraid.

BAZAROV I have something better for you. A job. My friend Gregor. I want you to turn him into a ... gentleman. Think of it as an interesting experiment ... Teach him to disappear into your world ...

PAVEL But why?

BAZAROV Just a notion ... But nevertheless, promise.

PAVEL No, I can't. Is there something else I can do for you instead. Anything.

KIRSANOV Pavel. That is the wish of a ... a man who is ... You can't refuse.

PAVEL But what about my beliefs. Doing what he asks would make a mockery of my life. I want Bazarov to go to his death knowing that I meant my life ... Bazarov. I still need your forgiveness. Will you give it to me.

BAZAROV For shooting me? Yes. For your beliefs? No.

[PAVEL *stands*]

PAVEL What you understand is what you come to believe in. That is the quality in life. And the comfort in death. God help us both.

[*He bows. Leaves*]

BAZAROV Arkady come here. Close to my mouth.

[ARKADY *bends down.* BAZAROV *begins to whisper in his ear*]

[FENICHKA *leads* SITNIKOV *in. He looks terrified*]

SITNIKOV Oh I don't know. I don't know how to behave. I've never

seen anyone die. I might do something inappropriate.
[BAZAROV *pushes* ARKADY *away. Sits up a bit*]

BAZAROV Oh my God. I'm dying? I'm dying? Why didn't anyone tell me!?
[SITNIKOV *looks around in horror*]

SITNIKOV Oh my God!

BAZAROV Oh my God!

SITNIKOV I'm sorry. So –

BAZAROV I'm dying. Did you hear him. I'm dying.

SITNIKOV Oh no. I thought he knew. Oh my God, this is awful. This is hell. I'm –

BAZAROV Viktor?

SITNIKOV Yes.
[SITNIKOV *leans close to him*]
[BAZAROV *leans back. Closes his eyes*]

BAZAROV Eeeeeeeee. [*Opens his eyes. Smiles*]

SITNIKOV Oh ... What. Oh. Yes ... a joke. Of course ... you're dying and you knew it all the time ... You'll be dead within the hour, you old joker ... I'm –
[*They all look at* SITNIKOV. *He sees this*]

SITNIKOV Sorry.

ARKADY We have to get out now. He asked to clear the room. [*to* KIRSANOV] Are the servants close at hand.

KIRSANOV Just outside.
[*They all start off. Except* ANNA, *who goes to a corner of the room, in the half-light, and watches* BAZAROV]

BAZAROV Arkady.
[ARKADY *stops*]

ARKADY Yes.

BAZAROV Stop there a moment. [*pause*] Seriously now, Arkady. What are you going to do with your life.

ARKADY Stay here for now ... Wait for Anna to make up her mind. Help my father manage things. The truth is I might belong here ... forever.

BAZAROV I liked our friendship ... very much. I found it useful.
[BAZAROV *holds out a hand.* ARKADY *takes it*]

ARKADY Are you afraid.

BAZAROV Well ... Oh yes. I am.

ARKADY I'll be back soon. Get some rest.
[ARKADY *leaves*]

The closing tableau of the CentreStage Company production

BAZAROV People are odd about death ... I'm not afraid at all ... Disappointed ... but not afraid. He'd want me to be though ... that would make me more human. Am I conscious ... Oh, I meant to ask someone to kiss my parents for me.

ANNA I'll do it.

BAZAROV Thank you ... Who said that.

ANNA Go to sleep.

[PIOTR, GREGOR, SERGEI, *and the* BAILIFF *come in*]

GREGOR They told us you wanted us in here, sir.

BAZAROV Yes.

GREGOR Is there something we can do.

BAZAROV Just stand there. Let me look at you all.

[*They look at one another*] Yes. I was right. You are the ...

[*He closes his eyes. Dies*]

[*Long pause*]

[PIOTR *goes close. Takes his pulse*]

PIOTR He's dead.

SERGEI We are the what. He didn't finish. We are the what.

GREGOR The future.

BAILIFF The dirt under his shoe.

GREGOR No the future.

BAILIFF Come off it. He was going to insult us something awful. One last great kick in the teeth.

SERGEI It's bad luck to be in the same room with a corpse if you don't have any coins in your pocket.

PIOTR Stupid man!

SERGEI You talking to me?

PIOTR It's superstitions like that that hold us all down, you moron.

SERGEI So you are talking to me, eh!! I'd watch out if I were you.

PIOTR Moron! Imbecile.

[PIOTR *leaves*]

BAILIFF That's it. That's what he wanted from us. A good fight! One last spectacle from the rabble before he kissed off. I tell you, we were the dirt in his fingernails!

[*He leaves*]

[GREGOR *shouts after him*]

GREGOR No! The future! [GREGOR *turns to* SERGEI] The future ... He told me. He took time and told me all about it. If I explain it to you, will you listen.

SERGEI I'll try.

[*Lights begin to fade*]

[ANNA *laughs. Sadly at first. Then with a kind of light joyful recognition*]

[*Brief blackout*]

[*Then flash back up to a dazzling white light which throws people into silhouette*]

[BAZAROV *has gone*]

[*All the other characters are on the periphery of the stage watching* GREGOR *and* SERGEI *walk off.* GREGOR *gesturing his explanation.* SERGEI *just listening*]

[*Blackout*]

[*End*]

Other published plays by George F. Walker

Ambush at Tether's End. In *The Factory Lab Anthology*
 (ed. Connie Brissenden). Vancouver: Talonbooks, 1974.

The East End Plays. Toronto: Playwrights Canada, 1988.
 Includes *Beautiful City, Better Living,* and *Criminals in
 Love.*

The Power Plays. Toronto: The Coach House Press, 1984.
 Includes *The Art of War, Filthy Rich,* and *Gossip.*

Rumours of our Death. In *Canadian Theatre Review* 25
 (Winter, 1980), pp. 43-72.

Science and Madness. Toronto: Playwrights Canada,
 1972.

Theatre of the Film Noir. Toronto: Playwrights Canada,
 1981.

Three Plays. Toronto: The Coach House Press, 1978.
 Includes *Bagdad Saloon, Beyond Mozambique,* and
 Ramona and the White Slaves.

Zastrozzi: The Master of Discipline. In *Modern Canadian
 Plays* (ed. Jerry Wasserman). Vancouver: Talonbooks,
 1985.

Editor for the press: Robert Wallace
Photos: Nir Bareket
Cover design: Gordon Robertson
Text design: Nelson Adams

For a list of our drama titles, or to
receive a catalogue, write to:

The Coach House Press
401 (rear) Huron Street
Toronto, Canada M5S 2G5